T0102484

Pretty Boy Detective Club

The Pretty Boy
in the Attic

By NISIOISIN

Translated by Winifred Bird

VERTICAL.

Pretty Boy Detective Club
The Pretty Boy in the Attic

Editor: Daniel Joseph

YANEURA NO BISHOUNEN

© 2016 NISIOISIN

All rights reserved.

First published in Japan in 2016
by Kodansha Ltd., Tokyo.

Publication rights for this English edition
arranged through Kodansha Ltd., Tokyo.

Published by Vertical, an imprint of
Kodansha USA Publishing LLC, 2021

ISBN 978-1-949980-88-2

Manufactured in the United States of America

First Edition

Kodansha USA Publishing LLC
451 Park Avenue South, 7th Floor
New York, NY 10016
www.readvertical.com

Pretty Boy Detective Club

The Pretty Boy
in the Attic

PRETTY BOY
DETECTIVE CLUB

NAGAHIRO
SAKIGUCHI

MAYUMI
DOJIMA

SOSAKU
YUBIWA

Illustration Kinako, Design Veia

MANABU
SOTOIN

MICHIRU
FUKUROI

HYOTA
ASHIKAGA

Rules of the Pretty Boy Detective Club

1. Be pretty.
2. Be a boy.
3. Be a detective.

0. Foreword

"I would gladly give ten years of my life if I could sit in front of this painting for two weeks on end, with only a crust of dry bread for food."

These words were supposedly uttered by Vincent van Gogh, who is, of course, one of the painters best-known in Japan. As for the painting he mentions in this legendary quote, which someone like me probably couldn't come up with even if she wracked her brains for a full ten years, I believe it was by Rembrandt. I wonder if, faced with that selfsame painting, a philistine like me would feel the way Van Gogh did.

Now, I'll take advantage of my claim to ignorance to admit that when I heard this quote, what it made me think of was that immortal masterwork we read in elementary school, *A Dog of Flanders*. You'd be hard pressed to find anyone who doesn't know the tragic tale of the young boy Nello and his dog Patrasche (make that "anyone in Japan," since apparently the novel is known only to a select few connoisseurs in its own country, if you can believe it). My elementary-school self wept just like everyone else over the last scene, in which the earnest Nello, who aspires to be a painter, is beckoned to heaven alongside his canine companion as he basks in the glory of the Rubens triptych he had always longed to see.

The tears were pouring down my cheeks.

But there is one questionable point in this tragic tale that the gloomy contrarian of a fourteen-year-old into whom that unpleasantly ingenuous elementary schooler transformed cannot bring herself to overlook. I do want to voice my doubts about the general morality of this tale of unrewarded virtue, in which Nello (a boy so poor he not only can't go to an exhibition of the one painting he most longs to see, but he even loses the very roof over his head) is honest enough to turn in some money he finds, only to die in obscurity without ever learning of the approbation of his own paintings. But the point I really can't get past is this: How did a boy who couldn't even afford food or shelter, who was standing at death's door along with his beloved dog, find the money to go see that painting?

I can hardly imagine that virtuous Nello and his dog, having just performed the beautiful act of returning some lost money, would be so morally inconsistent as to then sneak into the church where the painting hung without paying the cost of admission. But that, in fact, is the very conclusion the story leaves the reader to draw.

For years I've been wracked with guilt over the sin of harboring such a tactless objection to such a deeply moving tale of tragedy. So in the hopes that even if I couldn't expect a satisfying answer, I could at least share my pent-up feelings, I decided to make a clean breast of it—almost like going to confession (speaking of churches).

"…"

As usual, however, Sosaku Yubiwa, resident artiste of the Pretty Boy Detective Club, had nothing to say. In order to express his reticence in writing, I've taken the liberty of inserting an ellipsis as you see above, but the truth is that he didn't even give me—a year his senior— the courtesy of responding with silence.

He simply acted as if he hadn't heard my question, and kept staring at his canvas without so much as batting an eyelash—while he rubbed it with a piece of burnt toast, as if to say even a crust of bread is too good for barbarians who don't understand art.

What the hell is he doing with that toast, anyway? Feeding it to his painting?

At that point—perhaps because he couldn't bear the pitiful sight of me getting the cold shoulder from a younger club member, or perhaps because he had intuited the thoughts of the young artiste, and where had he even been up till now, anyway—the leader of the Pretty

Boy Detective Club popped out of seemingly nowhere with a laugh.

"Ha ha ha!"

As if he was laughing away my misery, or more likely, my foolishness.

"I myself shall give you a resplendent answer in Sosaku's stead. Needless to say, as a scholar of beauty, I, too, have heard this children's tale, but no such misgivings crossed my mind. And if the leader of a detective organization harbors no questions, then clearly no mystery is at hand. Obviously, some person of the church granted the boy and his dog their final wish—by secretly leaving the door unlocked."

Aha.

Such a tidy—or should I say beautiful?—interpretation left no room for argument or doubt.

Though if the one giving the explanation hadn't been our president, totally immune to logical argument as he is, I might well have stubbornly tried to argue the point. After all, if this person was motivated by kindness, then forget about leaving the door unlocked, surely they should have given the boy a crust of bread.

Then again, the man who painted *Sunflowers* would probably say that letting an aspiring artist see a painting is a far more charitable act than giving him some bread.

Perhaps dying in front of that painting had more value than living anywhere else.

It's a pretty convincing argument, coming from Van Gogh.

Why? Because even if it's unclear whether or not he really did spend two weeks in front of the Rembrandt he loved so much, the fact is that he shot himself sometime thereafter—which means that rather than ten years of his life, he gave his life itself.

1. The Club Is Called to Action

After class that day, I was getting ready to head to the art room as usual when the cell phone in the pocket of my slacks rang.

Coming to school in a boy's uniform had already earned me more attention from my classmates than the old me could ever have imagined, and now that ring was threatening to make me even more conspicuous. I answered, a shiver running down my spine.

"Ms. Dojima. You are being called to service as a member of the Pretty Boy Detective Club—please set aside any other plans you may have and report to the art room immediately," came the unilateral command from the other end.

Even over the phone, the vice president's beautiful voice lost none of its power to make me stand instantly to attention—but before I could reply, the line went dead.

This wasn't due to poor etiquette on the part of

Nagahiro Sakiguchi, known to the outside world as the popular president of the student council, but rather to the fact that I was so unfamiliar with my phone that I accidentally hung up on him.

Then, to make matters worse, I tried to use it like a walkie-talkie—*I don't know how to redial, over.*

I'm not sure how to put this.

Even though I'm a modern middle school kid, I lived a long time without a cell phone in order to protect my "overly good eyesight." Recently, however, one thing led to another and I ended up joining the Pretty Boy Detective Club, at which point I couldn't go phoneless anymore.

After all, weird as we may be, we're still a detective club.

A group, a team.

Which wouldn't work if we couldn't get in touch with each other in emergencies—and I suppose it's an unwritten rule that members should be reachable the rest of the time, too, emergency or no.

Well, the dos and don'ts of the Pretty Boy Detective Club tend to be pretty idiosyncratic, but anyway, when Sakiguchi found out that I didn't have a digital device, his response was, "Hehe. Don't worry, just leave it all to me."

When he gave me his word in that oh-so-persuasive voice of his—the voice that has earned him the nickname

Nagahiro the Orator, he of the beautiful voice—I found myself unable to press him for more details. But later, when I saw the item he'd provided for me, I felt like he'd hit me right where it hurts.

Right in my blind spot—the blind spot of my overly good eyes.

The reason I'd avoided using cell phones, and especially smartphones, in the past was that the light emitted by LCD screens is too strong for my sensitive eyes. On the flip side, using a cell phone that *doesn't* have an LCD screen poses no problem whatsoever.

So he gave me a kiddy phone.

Also known as a "safe phone"—one of those mobile devices that are small enough to fit in the palm of your hand, can't send texts, can only place calls to preset numbers, and basically don't have screens. Yup, no way this thing was going to affect my eyes.

In fact, it's so simple you could use it with your eyes *closed*—simpler even than a flip phone. You can't do much besides talk on it, though that actually makes it kind of a fitting phone for a detective.

Incidentally, since it was furnished by the club, they're covering the bills—and considering that the five numbers I can call all belong to the other members, not to mention the fact that one of those members is a rich kid with a bottomless savings account, I decided to accept their generosity.

As a long-time resident of the land of discommunication, I was pretty happy to have a phone, even if it was essentially a toy. But when I got calls like this summoning me to HQ with no concern whatsoever for my plans or opinions, I also felt like I'd had a dog collar put around my neck.

How do I put this?

When I was a kid, I thought that when communication systems got more advanced and everyone had computers, we'd all be able to live more independently, but now the future is here and it turns out we're more interconnected than ever.

Overconnected, you might say.

I guess human beings will never escape our communal nature, no matter how hard we try. With that sudden flash of insight, I hurriedly gathered my things to head home.

Home?

That's right, home.

When the last bell of the day rang, I'd been eager as could be to head to the art room, but now that I'd been "called up," I decided not to go—to the contrary, I made up my mind to rush back to the safety of home as quickly as possible, like I was fleeing a looming natural disaster.

Unfortunately, someone must have sussed out my operating principle ("If you're not invited, go anyway, but if you are, immediately decide you don't want to"), because when I got to the school gate, I found a sentry waiting there for me.

Kiboshed by the boshman. Er, bossman.

That would be Michiru Fukuroi, another member of the Pretty Boy Detective Club—if the universally loved councilman Sakiguchi was Yubiwa Academy's official representative, then the universally feared delinquent Fukuroi was its shadow representative.

Astonishingly, this king of the underworld spread his arms wide to block the likes of little old me.

"What the hell d'you think you're doing, Dojima? You call yourself Mayumi the Seer, but you look the other way when the president orders a meeting? Shit, I saw this coming a mile off!" he finished, glaring at me belligerently. Boy is he terrifying.

I definitely don't recall accepting Mayumi the Seer as my nickname, but this didn't seem like the right moment to raise that point.

Incidentally, we call him Michiru the Epicure, he of the beautiful palate.

Yes, you read that right, a rule-breaker who loves to cook.

Although "a cook who loves to break rules" might be more accurate.

Hang on, though, this order came from the president?

It was the vice president who had called me—but this went all the way to the top?

In that case, I wanted to go even less.

"Come on, get your ass in gear and come to the art room. You keep grumbling and I'll see to it you never work in showbusiness again."

"Uh, I don't think I belong in that world in the first place…"

The delinquent—who, despite being the very embodiment of the rebellious male middle school student, is meekly obedient to the leader and the leader alone—made a move to grab me by the collar.

Not so fast, buddy!

By snatching the glasses off my face, I honed my eyesight to a razor's edge and managed to dodge his grasp—then I made a break for it.

"You little shit! You're pretty sprightly for such a gloomy kid…"

Call me gloomy all you want—I'm free!

Why don't you skulk back to the school and look at your perfect face in the mirror!

But the next instant, the curtain fell on my little escape attempt—because no sooner had I given the delinquent the slip than something sideswiped me, hard.

"Oof!"

I thought for a moment that I'd been hit by a car (what a way to go, hit by a car while fleeing a beautiful boy), but as it turned out, it was neither a car nor a rugby player that flattened me—it was the first-year ace of the track team.

Otherwise known as Hyota the Adonis, he of the beautiful legs.

Another member of the Pretty Boy Detective Club—who had apparently been hiding behind a tree.

The fact that two members had been mobilized to capture a nobody like me spoke to the urgency of the president's summons.

"Ah ha ha. Nice try, Doji. You may have good eyes, but you'll never escape a boy who's faster than the speed of light!" chirped Mr. Bare-Legs as he pressed me into the asphalt—that's my secret name for him, by the way, since he's redone his uniform even more drastically than the delinquent by turning the slacks into short shorts. Even if the speed of light thing was an exaggeration, he was right that good eyes aren't going to help anyone run away from fast legs.

It was all over. Now that Mr. Bare-Legs was pinning me down with his bare legs, all I could do was steel myself for what lay ahead.

If I kept resisting, who knows where Mr. Bare-Legs might try to cop a feel in the confusion—just because I dress as a boy doesn't mean I've thrown my feminine virtue to the wind.

"Dammit, Dojima, stop making this so hard on us.

We've gotta hurry."

The delinquent pulled me to my feet.

Like he was pulling up a carrot.

I suppose being sandwiched between the bare legs of Hyota the Adonis and handled like a vegetable by Michiru the Epicure was something of an honor, but it still felt plain old humiliating.

"Oh, but if this is such an urgent matter, you should definitely feel free to go ahead and get started without me…"

"Stop acting like this has nothing to do with you. I bet you're one of those people who says, 'Everyone's always glued to their phones these days. I never see anyone reading on the train anymore!' If you'd just get out a book yourself, then there'd at least be one!" Accompanied by this dose of his usual somewhat overblown satire, the delinquent began dragging me back toward the school building.

To tell the truth, I probably could have found a window of opportunity to run away now that Mr. Bare-Legs had freed me from his bare legs, but the delinquent followed up his scathing satire by saying, "You sure as hell don't act like you're part of the team," and suddenly I didn't want to run anymore.

He wasn't treating me like part of a meal, he was treating me like part of the team.

Like I was one of them.

That was something I'd been even more starved for than a cell phone all these long years—Michiru the Epicure really did have a knack for serving up exactly what a person needed.

2. The Painting on the Ceiling

But just because the members of the Pretty Boy Detective Club were a team didn't mean they were mates. Some of them, like Sakiguchi the councilman and Fukuroi the bossman, even acted like sworn enemies in the outside world—the only place those two joined hands and took a seat at the same table was the art room.

The art room.

It fell out of use after Yubiwa Academy excised electives from its curriculum, until a band of rogues known as the Pretty Boy Detective Club commandeered it—and remodeled it to the point that it now bore no trace of its original appearance.

Luxuriously thick carpets covered the wooden floor, paintings and sculptures decorated every inch of wall, there were extravagant sofas, tables, and even a canopied bed—and when you flipped the switch beside the door, it wasn't a fluorescent light that flickered to life overhead but a pair of glittering chandeliers.

The place looked more like an art museum than an art room, but in fact it was the headquarters of the Pretty Boy Detective Club—they'd fixed it up to suit their tastes so they could spend their time in luxuriant comfort.

There could hardly be a less relaxing environment for someone like me, who had stubbornly failed to rid herself of her commonplace sensibilities, but apparently the original members still felt it to be lacking.

To make a long story short, this feeling seemed to be the reason for the urgent summons that day—because when the delinquent, Mr. Bare-Legs, and I arrived, we were greeted by the sight of the president and vice president holding a stepladder on which the child genius stood, his back arched and his arms outstretched as he flicked his paintbrush this way and that.

The president—Manabu the Aesthete, lover of beauty, aka Manabu Sotoin (elementary school year 5).

The vice president—Nagahiro the Orator, he of the beautiful voice, aka Nagahiro Sakiguchi (middle school year 3).

The child genius—Sosaku the Artiste, creator of beauty, aka Sosaku Yubiwa (middle school year 1).

For a second I thought they must be practicing for the annual Fire Brigade Parade or something, but no, the child genius seemed to be using the ceiling as a giant canvas—he was painting a mural on it.

Really now.

I'd been convinced the art room didn't have a speck of undecorated space left, but now even the ceiling, the sole remaining blank space, had fallen into their clutches.

A heartrending moment.

"Ah, there you are! A bit late, wouldn't you say, Michiru, Hyota, young Dojima? But never mind, I have faith that each of you did your very best. Thank you for coming!"

The president turned toward us, still holding onto the ladder.

Given that I'd done my very best to run away, I felt a twinge of guilt at this innocently warm welcome.

"My apologies for earlier, Ms. Dojima. For some reason the line went dead before I could be sure you'd gotten the message. I do regret inconveniencing you with my incompetence."

Sakiguchi's apologetic tone only added to my feelings of guilt, but they were somewhat assuaged when I remembered it was his unusual powers of imagination that were behind the purchase of my dog collar—the bastard had me tied up tighter than a cell phone contract.

As for the child genius up on the ladder, supported by the other two as he ran his brush across the ceiling, he didn't so much as glance in my direction—true, he probably would have fallen off if he'd tried to turn his head towards us while he was twisted into that unnatural position, but he was concentrating so intently that he seemed not even to have noticed our arrival.

From the looks of things he'd just begun painting, and I couldn't even begin to imagine what he had in mind, but his creative posture alone was enough to bowl me over.

"So, you finally got started on that ceiling redecoration project we've been tossing around—anything we can do to help?" the delinquent asked briskly, pulling the door shut behind him.

"For now, we could use another team member holding the ladder. It's still a little wobbly with just the two of us. And Sosaku could use an assistant to pass supplies up to him, plus we need someone to catch him on the off chance he falls. Positions, please."

"I wasn't asking you, Nagahiro. I was asking the president," the delinquent spat out at his rival, even as he stepped forward to hold the ladder.

That made sense strength-wise—my spindly arms hadn't gotten any more muscular just because I was dressed as a boy.

And the vaunted dynamism of Mr. Bare-Legs' legs was a natural fit for disaster management—if he did fall, the child genius would surely be in safe hands, or rather feet, just as I had been when Mr. Bare-Legs tackled me.

By process of elimination, that left me with the role

of assistant. It fell to me to pass the child genius the various brushes and paints lined up on the table, wipe away his sweat, and so on.

As a second-year student, seeing to the every need of a first-year evoked complex feelings for me, but oh well, if the student in question was Yubiwa, I could handle it—after all, as his last name suggests, he's the heir to the Yubiwa Foundation, the parent organization of our own Yubiwa Academy (he's the one with the aforementioned bottomless savings account, which means that for all intents and purposes he's the one actually holding my leash).

Yubiwa is way more of a VIP than the councilman or the bossman, so in a sense devoting myself to him was the best choice for my future—although here in the art room, he wasn't the heir to the Yubiwa Foundation, he was simply an artist and member of the Pretty Boy Detective Club.

I'd heard he was also the one behind most of the renovations in the art room—he's so impressively multitalented that he personally produced the vast majority of the replicas of famous paintings and sculptures on display.

"Um… Mr. President? Am I right in thinking that this is why we were urgently summoned here today?" I asked timidly, just to be sure.

"That is correct! Our task today as members of the

Pretty Boy Detective Club is to complete the art room at long last! The time has arrived!" Sotoin replied enthusiastically.

Honestly, his answer, seemingly devoid of hidden meaning as it was, came as a relief—don't get me wrong, it was a huge undertaking, and I couldn't forget that I was participating in the unsanctioned renovation of a school facility, but at least it had none of the over-the-top drama of certain other club activities I'd participated in, like flying halfway across the country in a helicopter, or sneaking into a rival school in the middle of the night; it felt more like a sitcom.

I was starting to feel not just relieved but even a little remorseful about my hasty attempt to escape the call to action. I decided I had overreacted—though as it turned out, this judgment was itself a bit hasty.

Not that I knew it at the time.

I had no way of knowing that this little redecoration project, seemingly the innocent product of the president's whims, would lead us back to a kidnapping that had taken place at Yubiwa Academy seven years earlier.

Yes, a kidnapping.

A strange and impossible crime, the likes of which I'd never even dreamed of.

3. Concerning the Pretty Boy Detective Club

Let's pause here for a brief explanation of the Pretty Boy Detective Club—which, if I were to remove myself from the equation for a moment, I would describe as a not-for-profit organization operating behind the scenes at Yubiwa Academy Middle School.

Being the wise and sensible person that I am, I was certain this organization couldn't possibly exist, despite plausible rumors to the effect that it was involved in just about all the trouble that went on at our school. Little did I know that its members were engaged day in and day out in solving "beautiful mysteries" from their headquarters in an art room long forgotten by students and teachers alike. Aside from me, the newbie, there are five of them:

Nagahiro Sakiguchi, the student council president; the bossman, Michiru Fukuroi; Hyota Ashikaga, the ace of the track team; Sosaku Yubiwa, heir to Yubiwa Academy—and the fearless leader of the Pretty Boy Detective

Club, Manabu Sotoin.

The leader is still in fifth grade, as it happens, and while the other members of the club dismiss it as "elementary," I personally think the question of how a fifth grader ended up commanding this distinguished group of middle schoolers is the biggest mystery of all. But we'll set that aside for now.

The hand of fate had led me to become a client of theirs, and thanks to a bewildering series of twists and turns, I ended up joining the organization myself. But even once I was a member, their activities seemed to me eccentric at best.

"Ha ha ha! Fear not, young Dojima, the very fact that you wished to join us is proof positive that you're plenty eccentric yourself!" the leader assured me, although his assurance was itself plenty worrying.

But compared to some of their activities, I had to admit that painting the art room ceiling without permission displayed a certain amount of moderation, if not restraint—not to mention the fact that it was already too late.

On the other hand, it was unclear why they'd decided to start on the ceiling at this particular moment— even if it was just a whim, there still must have been some spark, but oh well, probably not a question worth pursuing any further.

The work continued in silence for another hour or

so—and while I unfortunately can't say I performed the role of assistant very efficiently, I have no intention of taking full responsibility for that fact.

I mean, the child genius doesn't talk.

Since he remained mute and expressionless, giving no hint as to which brush or color he needed next, all I could do was guess.

Ordinarily, the leader—the only one of us able to glean anything about what goes on in Yubiwa's mind—would have interpreted for him, but today he had his hands full steadying the ladder.

Now that I think about it, the fact that both the president and vice president had taken on the humble role of ladder-holder shows what an excellent and sound organization the Pretty Boy Detective Club really is. For his part, Mr. Bare-Legs was lounging around taking it easier than any of us, but then, you generally want your emergency personnel to be as well-rested as possible.

I was just thinking that, thanks to the combined efforts of the three ladder-holders, the child genius was in no danger of falling—when.

4. Above the Ceiling

Kathunk!

One of the ceiling panels popped out of place.

The pressure from the child genius's brush had pushed it upwards into the crawl space above—with surprising ease, given that he was in an extremely awkward position and couldn't possibly have been pressing all that hard.

His brush, which thanks partly to our support had thus far been moving without so much as a moment's pause, suddenly stopped—though nothing registered on his ever-expressionless face.

"Ooh, he broke it, he broke it! Sosaku wrecked the art room!" Mr. Bare-Legs hooted.

Bad boy.

Anyone could see that the child genius hadn't broken anything—the panel was clearly made to pop out like that.

Even if they were in the same grade, though, given

the power and influence of the guy Mr. Bare-Legs was teasing, I had to admit he was also fearless.

"Did he? But what beautiful timing. Let's take a break. Come down from the ladder, Sosaku. And Michiru, get the tea and snacks ready."

The child genius and the delinquent silently obeyed the president's orders—neither of those unsociable characters seems the type to take orders from anyone, but with the leader they're both as docile as kittens.

While in physical terms my task may have been much easier than holding a ladder, serving as assistant to a genius artiste was mentally exhausting in its own right, so I was relieved at the chance for a break as well.

I'm not sure if the timing was beautiful per se, but I'll agree he punched through the ceiling at an opportune moment.

"Sakiguchi, do you think that ceiling panel was already damaged? If so, we'll need to fix it, which means we probably won't be able to finish the job today," I suggested obliquely (which is to say, blatantly), thinking that, since painting an entire ceiling in one afternoon was absurd to begin with, we should probably take this as a sign from above.

" ... "

The councilman peered into the gaping hole in the ceiling so intently that he appeared not to hear me.

What was that about?

Was he, as representative of the student body, concerned about damage to school property? Because pretty much anyone (except me) should be able to fix something like that easily enough.

"Oh no, Ms. Dojima, that is not my concern. It's just—that hole looks very much like the entrance to a secret passage."

A secret passage?

Once he said it, I could totally see why he might think that—it seemed less like a damaged old ceiling panel had given way, and more like a trapdoor had come open.

"Ya think so? So what does that mean, the art room had a loft?"

At first the delinquent's comment seemed way off-base, but actually it made a lot of sense—there probably wasn't anything as fancy as a loft above this classroom, but there could well be a secret room.

"Ha ha ha! I've always hoped there might be a door to a parallel world around here somewhere, but who would've thought it was right above our heads! To think, it was right under our noses this whole time!"

First of all, Mr. President, if it's above your head then it's not under your nose, and second of all, that went way beyond fancy to downright fanciful—though I guess if you're in fifth grade, searching for a tunnel to a parallel world isn't that weird?

I wondered what the child genius thought, given that he was the one who had opened the door to the tunnel, but he had sunk deep into the sofa and wasn't even looking at the hole—since his face is always expressionless, he didn't show any sign of exhaustion, but painting a mural on the ceiling seemed to be even more draining than watching someone else do it.

The genius's assistant may get tired, but the genius himself gets even more tired—or is that obvious?

That doesn't make me any less tired, though!

"Come on, guys, enough nonsense about lofts and parallel worlds. If there's anything up there, it's gotta be treasure," Mr. Bare-Legs said, his eyes sparkling.

Despite being the possessor of supernaturally beautiful legs that are the envy of every girl at Yubiwa Academy, his outlook is surprisingly realistic, so while I figured he was probably joking about the treasure, a hiding place did actually seem more plausible than a hidden room in terms of the way the school was laid out.

"Hmm. What do you think, Dojima?"

"Me?"

The delinquent's sudden question threw me off balance.

A newbie like me was supposed to give my opinion?

"Um, well… It could be littered with dead bodies, for all I know."

"Quit trying to scare us… And pick up after yourself

when you say something like that. Anyway, a picture is worth a thousand words. Standing around spitballing isn't getting us anywhere, let's climb up there and see what's what."

The delinquent put his foot on the ladder, and Saki-guchi casually reached out to steady it, so I reflexively ran to brace the other side.

I mean, he was definitely right that we'd find out more about what was up there by going to look than by talking about it—whether it was a loft, a parallel world, some treasure, or a pile of dead bodies.

Unfortunately, the delinquent was turned away at the door.

It wasn't his usual behavior that was the problem, but a simple question of size—because of the perspective, I hadn't been able to tell with my glasses on, but the hole-in-the-ceiling-slash-entrance was a bit too small for the delinquent, whose overgrown frame is a lot bigger than your average second-year middle school student's.

His head made it through, but his shoulders wouldn't fit.

I figured he'd still be able to get a glimpse of what was up there, but unfortunately it wasn't to be.

"It's pitch black. I can't see a thing."

"Uh-oh, that is a problem. Whatever can we do? Looks like we've hit a dead end. I'm sorry to say I don't have a flashlight on hand ... If only one of us were small

36

enough to fit *and* could see in the dark, but oh well."

"Get in there."

My clever attempt to avoid being given the job of investigating the hole seemed to have backfired, and all too soon I found myself in the delinquent's place.

If it were only a matter of size, either of the first-years—not to mention the leader, who was still in elementary school—could have fit through, but I suppose this was one of the few times when my eyesight would actually come in handy.

At the very least, it was a far more peaceful use for my eyes than seeing through scams at casinos—so I climbed up the ladder Sakiguchi and the delinquent were steadying for me, and slowly inched my way into the crawl space.

I'd never have managed something so tomboyish in a skirt, even with leggings on, but now that I was doing it, a current of excitement ran through me.

I felt like I'd *always* wanted to infiltrate the crawl spaces above our classrooms!

But as I took off my glasses in the unexpectedly cramped world above the ceiling, my excitement turned to disappointment.

This crawl space was just an ordinary crawl space.

There wasn't any hidden room, let alone something as fancy as a loft, and of course it wasn't connected to any fantastical magical worlds—plus there was no indication whatsoever of a treasure waiting to be discovered. It was just a cramped space not even a foot across, narrower than the entrance itself.

Since I'd rashly taken off my glasses and unleashed the full power of my vision, I saw every last detail of the thick layer of dust on the floor and the spiderwebs covering the walls, which gave me the creeps in addition to my feeling of disappointment.

It would be painful to deliver such a boring report to the denizens of the earthly world waiting so eagerly below, but for my own sake and theirs, I knew I had to get out of there—it seemed like just being in there could make a person sick.

Worrying that *I* might become the dead body in the crawl space, I somehow managed a one-eighty in that suffocating cranny—at which point the area that had previously been behind my back entered my field of vision.

Or, make that behind my legs.

Even my out-of-control eyesight doesn't allow me to see behind myself—which is not to say some sprawling world opened up when I turned around; the other side of the crawl space was just as cramped.

But, as if to emphasize just how cramped it was, a whole bunch of wooden boards were piled atop one another and jammed into the space opposite.

I wondered if someone had stuffed some leftover

lumber up there when the school was built, which would've amounted to one hell of a half-assed construction job, but that didn't turn out to be the case.

These were no ordinary boards, and they weren't lumber, either—they were nailed together into rectangular frames, with cloth stretched tightly over them.

In other words.

The crawl space was crammed with dozens of canvases.

5. Something Strange About the Paintings

Figuring it would be better to bring them along than to return empty-handed, I called down to the denizens of the world below and began handing them the canvases one by one—I passed them through the hole in the ceiling to the delinquent, who had a foot on the ladder, and he passed them to Sakiguchi.

There were just over thirty canvases in all, so it was quite a job, but I preferred doing it all at once to going back into that tiny space over and over.

I also thought that if we spent some time getting them down, then the child genius—who seemed utterly exhausted from the full exertion of his abilities—would be able to rest a little longer, which was an uncharacteristically thoughtful gesture coming from someone with a personality as lousy as mine.

I was starting to feel less like I was on an adventure or searching for lost treasure and more like I was giving the crawl space a much-needed spring cleaning, but I tried to put a positive spin on it by thinking that at least we'd discovered the door before the child genius had finished his mural.

Each canvas had a different painting on it, though clearly none of them were new—they'd been stored in just about the worst imaginable conditions, and every time I moved one, the paint flaked off or cracked. But I could tell they were mostly landscapes and still lifes.

I figured they must've been student projects from back when the art room was actually an art room, rather than the headquarters of a detective organization—thirty or so was just the right number for a class, and maybe when the room was shuttered, someone couldn't bear to throw the paintings away so they put them up in the crawl space?

That was about as far as my powers of deduction got me, but when I finally finished handing all the canvases down and climbed down the ladder myself, I found the others had reached a different conclusion.

They'd laid out the thirty-odd paintings on the rug, and without waiting for the return of the hardy explorer (me) or offering so much as a word of gratitude, they'd begun to inspect them—and despite my attempt to give him some rest, even the child genius had stood up from the sofa to take part, so I guess my good intentions were in vain.

So much for trying new things.

From now on, I'm doubling down on only thinking about myself.

In any case, now that the paintings had been laid out in the light, I realized I'd better secretly retract my as-yet-unvoiced theory about them being student projects.

My overly good eyesight had actually made it harder to tell, but now that I was out of that narrow space and back in the earthly realm with my glasses on, looking from the right distance with the right eyesight, it was clear they weren't the work of middle school students.

Even I, possessed of no eye for beauty at all when it comes to art, could see that whoever painted them had considerable skill.

If they *had* been painted by middle school students, then they must be from some golden age when every kid in the class was as gifted as the child genius—which seemed highly unlikely. If there had been such an age, I can't imagine Yubiwa Academy would've gotten rid of art class.

Suddenly, Mr. Bare-Legs' theory about a hidden treasure was seeming much more plausible. Could this be some sort of valuable art collection?

If so, who had the right to the paintings? Did I hold all rights as the one who found them, or would they be split between the six of us because I'd been investigating on behalf of the Pretty Boy Detective Club? If we did share, it would be only fair to divide the spoils

5:1:1:1:1:1, considering my outsized role in their discovery…

"Lemme guess, you're thinking up some petty scheme," the delinquent said, cutting into my thoughts with his razor-sharp insight.

How did he know?

Well, even if this were a "treasure," the horrible storage conditions must have lowered the value by at least half, and who would hide valuable paintings in the crawl space above a middle school art room anyway?

Apparently, though, I was the only one thinking about the value of the paintings, or to take it a step further, asset valuation—everyone else's attention was fixed elsewhere.

"Hey, Dojima. Don't these paintings look familiar?" the delinquent asked.

"Huh? Familiar?"

I took another look at the rows of paintings, which strictly speaking added up to three times ten plus three equals thirty-three—familiar? How could a pile of paintings that had been stashed away in the crawl space until a few minutes ago possibly look familiar…?

The truth was, not a single one rang a bell.

I canvassed my memory for any hint of familiarity, but came up empty—what I did find, however, was that there was something…uncanny about the canvases.

I'm not quite sure how to explain it other than by

saying they struck me as vaguely strange—but not all thirty-three of them.

Some were uncanny, and some weren't.

"I'd say about half of them feel kind of…unnatural," I muttered.

"Half? I'd say a third. Ten, maybe," the delinquent answered.

"I'm getting it from fully eighty percent of them."

"Twenty-two of 'em for me."

The councilman and track star added their impressions—was there a reason Mr. Bare-Legs' count was so precise? I knew I couldn't expect a comment from the silent genius, so now it was just a question of what our leader was thinking.

"Hm? I don't sense anything particularly odd about them. I simply feel that each and every one is truly beautiful!"

"…"

It struck me as highly questionable that the leader of a detective organization would utterly fail to sense the weirdness that even a newbie like me was picking up on—not to mention the wild indiscriminacy of summing up this pile of old, ragged, crumbling paintings as "truly beautiful."

Was this boy really Manabu the Aesthete?

What if he was just a frisky elementary student who called everything under the sun "beautiful"? A secret shiver of anxiety ran through me.

But setting that aside, and despite the variation in actual numbers, four out of six of us definitely sensed something odd about this mysterious collection of paintings—even if I couldn't explain where, exactly, that feeling came from.

"Hmm. They're not just familiar, it's more like déjà vu," the vice president mused. "Not so much a sense that something is wrong than that something is missing, perhaps."

If a gloomy type like me said something so roundabout and suggestive, everyone would almost certainly be annoyed, but when the guy with the beautiful voice said it, it sounded perfect. Annoyingly perfect.

Déjà vu. A sense that something's missing.

My meager mental dictionary couldn't really distinguish a sense of familiarity from déjà vu, but a sense of something missing sounded right, and I felt like we were getting closer to the truth—there was definitely something lacking from these paintings.

Lacking.

It wasn't painterly passion or technique or anything like that, but something more concrete—

At that moment, a gunshot rang out behind me.

6. The Artist's Eccentricity

Sorry, I was wrong about the gunshot. My bad.

I wasn't used to the sound so I misidentified it, but I doubt any other modern middle school girl would make the same mistake—which is to say, what I actually heard was the ersatz shutter click a smartphone makes when you take a picture.

You know, *Kachak!*

A sound the kiddy phone they gave me would never make in a million years.

Anyway, the photographer was none other than the child genius.

He was pointing the lens on the back of his phone at the rows of paintings, and clicking away like a tourist snapping pictures of some famous landmark.

It seemed like he was planning to photograph each of the thirty-three paintings.

"Y-Yubiwa, what are you doing?" I asked, but he didn't answer.

Since he never answers his senior club member (me), I had a hard time telling whether he was ignoring me because he was focused on his photography, or just plain ignoring me.

"Ha ha ha. Be patient, young Dojima. Sosaku appears to have something in mind."

If the president says so, then patient I will be.

At the very least, Sosaku was more likely to have something in mind than the president, who never seems to have anything in his mind at all—hmm, maybe by taking pictures of the paintings and converting them to digital data, he could perform an image search online?

And then he might be able to figure out who'd painted them?

As far as I could tell when I was passing them down from the crawl space, none of them were signed on either front or back (which further weakened my theory that they were student works someone couldn't bear to throw away), but if we could identify the artist, that information might well offer a clue as to why they seemed so strange.

It might also help determine their value (I still hadn't discarded the "hidden treasure" theory—in contrast to Mr. Bare-Legs, who'd suggested it in the first place but seemed to have forgotten about it completely. Did that mean he didn't want his share?).

But once the child genius was done photographing

the paintings, his next move wasn't anything so high-tech as a digital image search.

On the contrary, it was startlingly analog.

Pulling out a felt-tip pen from who knows where, he abruptly began writing on the screen of his smart-phone—what the hell was this kid doing?!

I rushed over, intending to put a stop to his eccentric behavior, but the leader halted me in my tracks, repeating, "Be patient, young Dojima. Sosaku appears to have something in mind."

"And you appear incapable of saying anything else!!"

Whatever the child genius had in mind, I wouldn't call writing directly on the screen of your phone the act of a sane person. I could maybe understand if he were using a stylus, but the writing utensil in the child genius's hand was far more primitive than that.

Just because LCDs are my natural enemy, that didn't mean I could overlook this act of wanton vandalism—but while I was dealing with the leader, Yubiwa seemed to have finished his "drawing."

First the ceiling, now an LCD—I was starting to wonder if this guy just drew on everything, but when he turned his phone toward me, I realized what was actually going on.

His intention became immediately obvious.

Needless to say, he wasn't showing the screen to me specifically, he was showing it to Sotoin—but anyway.

"O—Ohhhhh! Oh oh oh!"

My voice rang out before I could stop it. Not a very beautiful one, either.

This truly was a case of a picture being worth a thousand words.

Or perhaps I should say, of one glance being enough.

The photo the child genius had pulled up on his screen was of the painting at the far end of the row—with his line drawing overlayed on it.

It was a quick sketch, so it wasn't very detailed, but all the same I could make out several figures bent forward—

"It's Millet's *The Cleaners*!" I blurted out.

"*The Gleaners*, I believe," Sakiguchi corrected curtly, dampening my high spirits.

Come on, man, read the room.

Any confusion over the name is probably just a question of translation anyway, so we'll set that aside. The point is, the painting was that famous work by the French master—except that *the human figures* had been removed from the frame.

Simply put, the artist had taken the same viewpoint as Millet, but had *only painted the scenery*.

It was only natural that we had a sense of déjà vu, that we felt like something was missing.

What was missing was the people.

I guess the child genius had realized this right away,

and run with the eccentric idea of drawing on his phone in order to run it by the rest of us.

True, his method revealed the truth at a glance, but I'm pretty sure a few words would've sufficed to achieve the same effect… Does he really hate talking that much?

Anyway, a single example was enough.

He didn't need to deface his screen any further (would the ink even come off? Though I guess for someone with his economic resources, a smartphone might as well be a portable whiteboard)—we could assume the situation was the same for the other thirty-two paintings.

A second look confirmed it.

The sense of familiarity, of oddness, of déjà vu, of something missing, it all made sense now.

That painting over there was *The Swing* by Fragonard, but without the people.

That one was *Ophelia* by Millais, but it was just the background.

That one was Manet's *The Luncheon on the Grass*, but again, no people.

That one was Renoir's *Dance at Le moulin de la galette*. But no people.

The same contrivance had been applied to paintings by Picasso and Dalí, Botticelli and Van Gogh, even one of Hokusai's masterpieces.

These weren't landscapes and still lifes, they were paintings that had been *turned into landscapes and still lifes*—it was so simple, I couldn't believe I hadn't seen it sooner.

A pitch-perfect solution. Or make that a picture-perfect one.

Once that became clear, it also became clear why each of us had gotten a weird feeling from *a different number* of the paintings—the spread reflected our familiarity or lack thereof with the classic paintings these works were based on.

Since I had said half of them looked odd, that meant I had some knowledge of sixteen of the thirty-three paintings, give or take (even if I didn't necessarily know the names of the original paintings or their creators)—conversely, I couldn't feel like something was missing from the remaining sixteen or seventeen paintings because I wasn't familiar with the sources.

The fact that the delinquent only thought ten of them looked odd meant that he only knew a paltry ten of the original paintings, compared to my sixteen.

"Yesss! I beat the ignorant delinquent!"

"Dojima, your brain filter is off," he sighed. "Your true colors are starting to show"—but let him say what he wants.

It doesn't make him any less of a loser.

When I asked him which ones he'd recognized, though, most turned out to be ones I hadn't known—so maybe it's more accurate to call him a niche enthusiast than an ignoramus.

That stinks.

Anyhow, I could see how the highly cultured student council president would recognize eighty percent of the paintings, but it was a real surprise that Mr. Bare-Legs—whose only brush with culture was probably in his morning yogurt—recognized twenty-two of them, a full two-thirds.

Even if the reason he gave such a specific number was just that his knowledge was more concrete and less nebulous than my own, still, I was amazed to find his appearance belied not only unexpected athleticism but intellect as well.

As clever as he is beautiful, it seems.

"Uh, I'd hold off on the praise if I were you. Look, classic paintings are, like, all nudes. So I just end up absorbing the knowledge while I'm checking out the ladies."

Yeah, forget the praise.

And he has the nerve to say it with that adorable, bashful smile!

But he was right, a lot of the originals these paintings were based on did feature naked women—so I suppose Mr. Bare-Legs started with a leg up on the competition (not that it's a competition).

"I'm no match for Nagahiro, though. Guess dragging your first-grade fiancée to the museum every day pays off."

"Hyota. I do not drag her to the museum every day. Please refrain from saying things that could be misinterpreted," the councilman scolded him sharply. But he does do it every month or so, from what I hear—so I nonchalantly took a few steps back, putting a little distance between myself and the dangerous individual.

The taciturn child genius hadn't revealed how many he knew, but I wouldn't be surprised if he'd recognized all thirty-three paintings from the start, given that it's his area of expertise—we were busy wracking our brains, but he probably hadn't even seen it as a mystery.

The problem, however, was our leader.

Who'd recognized none.

I suppose that's understandable enough for a fifth grader, but come on, he should at least know one!

"Unfortunately, you see, my mind is untrained—though my aesthetic eye is not."

"Aren't we talking about aesthetic eyes right now?"

Though he did say they were all beautiful, come to think of it, which I suppose qualified as discerning in its own way—after all, they were all based on timeless masterpieces.

Of course, I'm sure they wouldn't measure up if you compared them to the originals.

Even without the effects of their poor storage conditions, subtracting all the people from great paintings was something of a debasement. At the very least, it couldn't possibly be an improvement.

"Or is this a standard exercise for painters? They say all art begins with imitation, and I guess filling in the landscape where the humans used to be takes a certain skill…" I tacitly directed this at the child genius, only to be tacitly ignored—my suspicion that the younger student hated me seemed more credible every day.

"In my admittedly limited experience, I've never heard of any such exercise," Vice President Sakiguchi, the conscience—or perhaps the criminal—of the Pretty Boy Detective Club replied in his stead. "By the by, the reproduction of famous artwork is strictly prohibited by law in some instances. One is not permitted to use the same size canvas as the original, for example."

Very thorough of him to round out his response with an added bit of trivia.

Was that because some copies were so perfect that they couldn't otherwise be distinguished from the originals? Though that didn't apply to these paintings, of course—they had become entirely different works of art.

But then again, the quality was so high that it seemed unlikely they were done for practice. They would only look inferior if we placed them next to the originals.

And there was the real puzzle.

Why in the world had the artist created these strange

54

paintings, and so many of them at that?

"Hmm... It's almost as if the people imprisoned in the locked rooms of these canvases have all made a dramatic escape!" Sotoin exclaimed, his imagination running wild.

A true mental athlete.

Or would that be aesthete?

Though "locked room" did sound very much like something the leader of a detective club would say.

Then again, even though a canvas is certainly a sort of locked room, they'd vanished from the places they belonged, which really made it less like an escape... and more like a...

"Should we assume there was only one painter?" Sakiguchi asked of no one in particular.

"I sure as hell hope there aren't more than one of these weirdos out there!"

The delinquent's response was pure emotional reaction, but yeah, I had to agree.

"Wow, that's the first time we've ever agreed on anything."

"Cut the shit, Dojima. You're not my rival."

Damn, that was cold.

"You have a point, Michiru. The artist's unique touch gives it away—I'm sure these paintings are as close as possible to the originals, but they share a certain character that can't be concealed," the leader said, like he was suddenly some expert on painting. His reliability was highly questionable, though. "Why make these paintings, and why hide them in the crawl space? Ah, how delightful! An endless font of mysteries!"

"But Sotoin, regardless of how many artists there were, how can we ever find out the answers to those questions?"

We'd ended up with an impromptu art show, but I thought we were lucky just to have been able to figure out why the thirty-three canvases had seemed so weird.

No way we were going to be able to pin down the details of these paintings that had been hidden away in the crawl space for…conservatively, I'd say three years, at the very least.

"Hmm. Then let us turn our attention to a different mystery."

"A different mystery?"

There were more?

Apparently, the mysteries really *were* endless.

"Don't tell me it's another beautiful one," I said, a tad sarcastically.

"No, you could call this mystery the very opposite of beautiful—and yet we absolutely must investigate it," Sotoin replied bewilderingly.

The opposite of beautiful?

But we still had to investigate?

The real mystery was what in the world he was

talking about.

"What do you mean, Mr. President?" asked Mr. Bare-Legs, who seemed as confused as I was.

"We will table the question of why the artist painted these pictures for the moment—but as for the question of why the artist didn't paint *that* picture, well, that is a mystery the Pretty Boy Detective Club must face," Soto-in replied.

That painting? What painting?

"The most famous painting in the world, so famous even an uneducated fellow like me knows it: Leonardo da Vinci's *Mona Lisa*." Sotoin cocked his head before continuing. "A student of beauty such as myself simply cannot accept that the artist painted so many canvases without including the *Mona Lisa*."

7. The Unpaintable Painting

Now that he mentioned it...

There didn't appear to be a painting based on the *Mona Lisa* among the thirty-three canvases lined up in the art room.

"What's the problem with that, Mr. President? Plenty of other paintings didn't make the cut. Like Munch's *The Scream*, for example."

The delinquent had put my own thoughts into words, but at the same time, I did kind of see where Sotoin was coming from.

If you were selecting thirty-three masterworks from the history of art, would anyone really leave out the *Mona Lisa*?

Of course, everyone has their preferences, and the world's a big place, so I suppose there must be someone out there who refuses to acknowledge the artistic value of the *Mona Lisa*.

The delinquent's example of *The Scream* was just one

of countless other paintings the artist hadn't chosen—it wasn't like the *Mona Lisa* was the only one.

That was all well and good from an objective perspective—but the truth was, as a member of the Pretty Boy Detective Club, I did feel it was odd that the one painting known even to our leader, Manabu the Illiterate, sorry, the Aesthete, hadn't been included in the collection.

Again it felt like something was missing.

"…Perhaps we can use that omission as a clue to deduce the identity of the artist," the vice president said, seeming to choose his words with care. "As far as I can see, these thirty-three paintings represent a wide variety in terms of both era and technique. We have landscapes, nudes, abstracts, portraits, genre paintings, historical paintings, war scenes, Japanese paintings, ink wash paintings… There appears to be no unifying characteristic whatsoever—but if we carefully analyze the criteria by which these paintings were selected, I do believe our chances of arriving at the identity of the artist are quite high."

Really?

I couldn't help feeling skeptical, but on the flip side, even Sakiguchi the strategist could see no other lead worth pursuing.

Well, it was definitely true that if we figured out who the painter was, we'd solve all the other mysteries at the same time—the paintings may have been old, but it wasn't like we'd dug them up from an ancient tomb or something.

Most likely the artist was still alive, which meant once we identified him or her, we should be able to get the story straight from the horse's mouth. Even if they weren't student projects, the fact that they were stored in the crawl space above the art room meant the artist must have some connection to Yubiwa Academy.

And if the artist was connected to Yubiwa Academy, then we could probably go through the child genius to get in touch, seeing as he was heir to the school's parent organization—just as I was starting to see a glimmer of hope for our investigation, a sound chimed out over the speakers, one of the few remaining signs that this thoroughly redecorated art room was actually still a classroom.

It was the bell signaling that everyone had to leave the school.

"Well, sounds like it's time to wrap up. That's enough for today. Please continue contemplating the problem for homework."

"Really? We can go home already?"

The leader's words caught me so off guard that I accidentally let slip my secret desire to leave—ordinarily, this bunch of scofflaws who called themselves the Pretty Boy Detective Club gleefully ignored the bell that sent everybody home.

The very fact that they'd commandeered the art room was itself against school rules, and I myself had spent the better part of the night with them in this room on previous occasions—not to mention that the mere presence of our elementary school leader on middle school grounds violated the Yubiwa Academy code of conduct.

But now the members of that very same club were trotting off home just because the bell had rung? Since when were we an association of good little boys and girls?

Normally the end-of-the-day bell was no more than a reminder that it was time for dinner—and I'd secretly been dying to see what the delinquent, aka Michiru the Epicure, was going to treat us to today!

I'd never been so disappointed in my life!

And now Sotoin was giving us homework?

But the Pretty Boy Detective Club is no democracy—for this group of good little outlaws, the leader's word is absolute.

"Well, we can't finish the mural until we do something about these bizarro paintings anyway. Guess I might as well try using my brain for once."

"A fine idea. For my part, I will use my authority as student council president to investigate on the school end of things—perhaps something happened when the art room was shuttered."

"I think I'll pull a couple art books off the shelf at home and have a look at the originals. It's been a while, and comparing them with the copies might help me figure something out. Taking the nudes out of nude paintings is a serious crime! It's unforgivable!"

Mr. Bare-Legs seemed to be motivated by something slightly different from the rest of us, but I realized that at this point, objecting would be futile.

Purely in terms of personal benefit, I wouldn't get anything out of putting up a fight right now—because if I said I didn't give a damn about these weird paintings and we might as well stuff them back in the crawl space and get on with the mural, and for some reason they actually listened to me, I'd be forced back into my miserable position as artist's assistant.

And depending on how things went, that could take all night.

No joke.

Whatever change had taken place in the mind of our leader, I figured I'd better take advantage of it and go home if he'd let me—I was only kicking the can down the road, but maybe, just maybe, tomorrow after class I'd manage to slip past the delinquent and Mr. Bare-Legs and make my escape.

"For once, our resident contrarian seems to be without an objection. It's decided then!"

The leader clapped his hands to punctuate his words.

Apparently they called me "our resident contrarian" behind my back—well, the name does fit.

Just then, I realized we hadn't heard the child genius's opinion yet. Of course, it was customary for the silent artist (who was particularly silent toward me) to keep his thoughts to himself in situations like this, but that custom also included our telepathic leader sometimes expressing the child genius's thoughts for him.

Did that mean the leader was taking advantage of the child genius's silence to ignore his opinion? Speaking as someone who was regularly ignored by the child genius, turning the tables on him like that would give me a certain sense of satisfaction. On the other hand, since Sosaku the Artiste was the linchpin of this particular investigation, as the discoverer of the paintings it made me wince a little.

Knowing him, he probably didn't care one bit for a bunch of old canvases and just wanted to get on with painting the ceiling—but if so, shouldn't I fulfill my role as "our resident contrarian" after all?

The thought of not going home broke my heart, but I honestly did want to see him finish the mural.

Bearing witness to the birth of a magnificent work of art, and assisting in its completion, would bring joy even to a twisted human being like me—well, a little, anyway.

That's why I was about to stop the leader, who was

already gathering his things to go, as well as the delinquent, the councilman, and Mr. Bare-Legs—when I realized something.

Wait.

Wait, wait, wait.

What if I was wrong—what if his thoughts had already been expressed?

What if Sotoin had already told us the child genius's opinion—what if he, more than anyone, actually wanted to investigate the true nature of the canvases we'd discovered?

What if the reason Sotoin's early dismissal seemed so uncharacteristic was that it was in fact the child genius who had suggested we investigate the problem as a homework assignment?

I turned toward Yubiwa.

But he was expressionless as ever, and even with my glasses off, I couldn't decipher his thoughts.

Nor his wishes.

8. The Road Home

To my great relief, the delinquent and Mr. Bare-Legs walked me home. If I wanted to be treated like a girl I wouldn't dress like a boy, but the sun was setting early these days, so I decided to take them up on their offer—though being boxed in between the two of them felt more like an arrest than a rest for my overanxious mind.

"I doubt anything untoward will happen, but in light of recent events, there's no harm in taking a few precautions," Sakiguchi had declared. I'd been pulled into trouble of all sorts and sizes since joining the Pretty Boy Detective Club (most of which originated with the club's own members), so I wasn't exactly sure which "recent events" he was referring to, but if it had to do with my route home, my guess was he was referring to the case involving Kamikazari Middle School.

"Though things're probably so screwed up over there that they don't have time to mess with our school," the delinquent countered, before nevertheless delivering me to my doorstep—which I was grateful for in terms of my personal safety, but since my parents seem to be keeping a closer eye on me lately, the situation was a bit delicate.

How did they feel, I wonder?

Was it easier for them to sleep at night when their daughter had been dreaming her life away chasing a non-existent star, or now that she dressed like a guy and spent her time with a bunch of colorful pretty boys?—I had a feeling it was six of one, half a dozen of the other.

"Actually, we came along more for your peace of mind than for actual protection. No matter how vigilant you are, if someone wants to kidnap you, they're gonna kidnap you," Mr. Bare-Legs said with an incongruously innocent smile—I guess people who've been kidnapped three times really do have a different perspective.

"Maybe that's why Nagahiro wanted you to have a cell phone."

Huh, interesting.

I'd been certain the sly councilman was trying to keep me on a short leash, but sure enough, kiddy cell phones can function as personal alarms, too.

The sole way in which this thing outdid the latest smartphone technology was that if you pulled on the strap, a really loud alarm went off.

"Hmm… Do you really think Sakiguchi took all that into consideration?"

"Yup. A little overprotective, if you ask me, but

worthy of a guy with a lolicon. Naturally he's an expert on kid's cell phones."

"Worthy" isn't exactly the word I'd use, but...

I had mixed feelings about being treated not just like a girl but a little girl, but oh well, I might as well accept that overprotectiveness as a positive thing.

Wait a second, though—kidnapping?

Speaking of kidnapping.

"Hey, you guys," I said as I was about to shut the front door. "Sotoin said it was like the people imprisoned in the locked rooms of those thirty-three canvases had made a dramatic escape, but don't you think it's more like they were kidnapped?"

"Huh?"

The delinquent looked at me dubiously.

But Mr. Bare-Legs, with his abundant experience of being kidnapped, seemed to understand my point straight away.

"Yeah, you could be right. It's not so much that they were shut up in those pictures and escaped—it's more like they were being protected by the pictures, but got abducted... That sounds right to me."

"What's the difference?"

The delinquent still didn't seem to get it.

Figures, since he's never been kidnapped!

I mean, since the bossman would be more likely to kidnap someone than be kidnapped, maybe he had a hard time grasping the niceties.

"What do you think I am, some kind of monster…?" The delinquent glared at me. "Whatever. You better give this some serious thought tonight. The leader told us this was homework."

Funny how you don't know the difference between escaping and being abducted, but you can see right through my laziness.

"Ah hah! I think you like me!" I crowed.

"I'm gonna kill you."

So hard to find that sweet spot of familiarity.

Note to self: never forget that when you leave the art room, these guys aren't your friends.

I may be gloomy, but I tend to get carried away, and one day that's going to get me in trouble.

"Seriously though, Dojima, you can't expect us to treat you like a guest forever. I've said this a million times, but you gotta start seeing yourself as a member. What are you, one of those trending celebrities who makes a guest appearance as a voice actor in the movie version of a hit anime?"

I was flattered that he would compare a person like me to a trending celebrity, but boy oh boy, the satire was scathing tonight.

"Give it a rest, Michiru. That kind of talk might come back to bite us when they decide to turn our exploits into a movie."

For once, Mr. Bare-Legs took a scolding tone—which was in itself a fine thing, but man are his ambitions over the top.

Give up on the movie version already.

On the other hand, the delinquent had a point.

And if a delinquent was giving me a lecture, I knew I was in trouble.

I promised the two of them that I'd come up with a theory to present by the end of the school day tomorrow, and shut the door with a sigh of relief.

A theory.

It was time for what we detectives call some deduction.

This was going to be rough.

It's a bit late to admit this now, but I'm not much for reading detective novels—actually, books aren't really my thing in general. Yes, I'm one of those people responsible for reducing the number of readers on trains.

I said a quick hello to my family, then went to my room and took off my boy's clothes—the uniform itself was comfortable enough for a girl to wear, but I still wasn't used to having my chest bound like that.

I was dying to take it off the instant I got home.

The outfit I was wearing was one I'd altered in imitation of the clothing the child genius had tailored for me—though of course I'm no costume artist, and as a total novice I had only managed a faint echo of what he'd achieved.

Look and learn.

All art begins with imitation.

Our current view was that the thirty-three canvases we'd discovered weren't practice exercises—and yet it was equally clear that the mysterious artist hadn't intended to produce counterfeits.

Which left us with …

I mulled over the problem as I did a quick costume change from boy to girl. Throwing on something to lounge around in didn't require much mulling over, so I had plenty of leeway to focus my thoughts elsewhere.

Deduction while dressing.

The only idea I could come up with was that the paintings were meant as some kind of critique.

Satire in the delinquent's vein, if you will.

A message.

By intentionally altering universally acclaimed masterpieces, the artist was trying to put across some idea … Given that their quality was so high I couldn't even imagine how the artist had managed to paint them in the first place, maybe it had been a little harsh to call it a debasement, but still, it was unquestionably desecration. After all, each of those original paintings was somebody's baby.

If I started with the hypothesis that these pictures were intended as some kind of gauntlet thrown down to the great painters of yesteryear, I felt like I could scaffold some deductions onto that by the end of the day tomorrow—but I decided to stop thinking about it for the time being.

My deductions might do for a jury-rigged hypothesis based on limited information, but mere deductions weren't going to cut it here.

Maybe they would fly if I belonged to an ordinary detective club, but I didn't. I was a member of the Pretty Boy Detective Club.

My deductions had to be beautiful.

"Be pretty, be a boy, be a detective, is it?" I muttered to myself.

Those were the rules of the club.

And then there was the *fourth rule*, the one I needed to permanently etch into my mind in huge block letters—

As if on cue, just as I finished changing, a sound rang out from the pocket of my uniform where it sat on the hanger.

My kiddy phone was ringing.

What the heck? Don't tell me the leader was summoning me again, just when I'd finally returned to the refuge of home and was lazing around in my pajamas! Apologies to Sotoin, who was kind enough to treat me like every other member of the club despite the fact that I was not only the newbie, but a grumpy girl and not even a pretty boy at all—but I was genuinely fed up.

For a second, I waffled over whether I should pretend I hadn't heard it, but I knew that wouldn't fly.

I steeled myself and pressed ANSWER.

But my mental preparations turned out to be unnecessary.

To put it another way, the attack came from a completely unexpected direction, an ambush for which I was thoroughly unprepared—because even though only the members of the Pretty Boy Detective Club were supposed to know my phone number, the person on the other end of the line wasn't one of us.

"Hello, Ms. Dojima? It's me."

That voice.

The voice of the very person the overprotective Sakiguchi was trying to protect me from by giving me this kiddy phone.

"It's Lai Fudatsuki. You probably don't remember me."

Don't remember you? How could I forget?

9. Competing Theories

The following day after school, the members of the Pretty Boy Detective Club gathered in the art room as agreed. Strictly speaking, I—having not learned my lesson the previous day—attempted once again to escape, but was captured all too easily by the lethal combination of Mr. Bare-Legs and the delinquent.

Two straight losses.

Never mind my membership in a detective club and the whole "Mayumi the Seer" thing, I ought to do something about this hopelessly twisted personality (the one that makes me not want to go somewhere the moment I'm actually invited) purely for my own sake—but anyhow, there we were around the table.

The door to the crawl space was still hanging open, and the thirty-three paintings were still lined up neatly in rows—and the ceiling mural, too, quietly awaited its completion.

"Well then! Let the presentation of theories begin! I

haven't the slightest doubt you will entertain me royally, lads!"

The leader made no attempt to hide his effervescent excitement—but to be honest, my confidence started to waver in the face of such high expectations.

To calm myself, I took a sip of the tea the delinquent had poured me.

"Ptooey!"

I spit it out. It was too delicious.

Wasn't this supposed to be a blend he made specially to suit my lowbrow palate?!

"Woops, my bad. Got 'em mixed up," the delinquent said calmly, wiping the table clean with the practiced hand of a seasoned waiter, using a cloth he just happened to have at the ready—the sure sign of a premeditated crime.

Was this my punishment for trying to escape two days in a row? Or maybe he was getting back at me for being too flip with him lately?

Either way, I was reminded of just how terrifyingly foolhardy it was to make an enemy of the guy in charge of the food—though thankfully, the whole thing had the unexpected benefit of releasing a bit of my tension.

None of the other members showed any real sign of nerves, least of all the delinquent, who seemed quite cheerful now that he'd had his revenge.

Mr. Bare-Legs was lounging upside down on the sofa in his signature pose, his beautiful legs on full display, while as always, the child genius's blank face displayed no hint of his thoughts.

As I gazed at him, I started to wonder if I'd been overthinking the situation the day before, and maybe he really did just want to get on with the mural—as for Sakiguchi, well, I suppose he seemed quieter than usual.

Nagahiro the Orator typically acted as master of ceremonies when the whole club gathered, but this time he seemed to be hanging back.

Or was I imagining things?

I was probably just feeling guilty that only last night I'd been talking on the phone with his sworn enemy, the one and only student council president of Kamikazari Middle School.

Or maybe that was just what I wanted to think, because whenever Sakiguchi was acting weird, it meant something bad was coming down the pipeline—but anyway, after the delinquent waiter finished laying the table with an English-style afternoon tea of scones, fruit, and sweets, it was time to present our homework assignments.

I figured there would be some question as to who would present first, but that didn't turn out to be the case.

"I'll take the liberty of starting with myself! Please listen quietly as I present my deductions! I'd hate to rain on everyone's parade by solving the mystery straight off, but if I do, I hope you'll all shout 'Cowabunga!'"

Sotoin surprised me by taking the initiative to go first—though maybe I shouldn't have been so surprised. Whatever it was that made him lead the charge at times like these was precisely what gave him the generosity of spirit to lead this group of problem children.

I'd love to follow his example, if that were the kind of thing a person could emulate.

… Although the quality of his reasoning was another matter entirely.

"Yesterday, we concluded that the thirty-three paintings lined up over there were historic masterpieces recreated without the people, but I have since reconsidered. What if the opposite were actually true? What if the paintings we discovered yesterday were made first, and the famous masterworks on display at museums around the world were based on these canvases sitting here before us?!"

For a second my mouth dropped open at his outrageously bold theory, but then I came to my senses and thought, *No, not a chance.*

Sorry, no "Cowabunga!" for you.

Not that I'd have said it anyway, since I'm not a surfer.

True, the canvases had aged quite a bit thanks to their poor storage conditions, but there was no way they were centuries old. My guess was they were a decade old, at most.

On the off chance—the off off off chance—that these paintings actually had inspired various historic masterpieces, what would such valuable items be doing stored together in the crawl space of a random middle school?

"I commend you on your superb deduction, Mr. President. Such a twist brings to mind the epic reversals in the classic mystery novels of yesteryear," announced the heretofore reticent Sakiguchi, applauding as he spoke—though while you'd never guess it from his matchless voice, I'm fairly sure he didn't mean it as a compliment.

It almost sounded like he was making fun of the leader.

But the staunchly loyal vice president wouldn't make fun of the leader even if hell froze over, so I guess Sakiguchi had just reacted reflexively, like his attention was somewhere else.

Then again, it was also somehow unimaginable that the vice president would listen to the president's deductions (no matter how off the mark) with anything less than his full attention... So was he up to something after all?

I could only hope it was a merry surprise...

"Thank you, thank you! If so many artistic innovations did indeed originate here in this very art room, then I, as president of the Pretty Boy Detective Club headquartered here, would be filled with pride. My only regret is that my theory does not explain the absence of the *Mona Lisa* from this collection, but if we assume that Leonardo da Vinci once studied at this very school, then everything falls into place."

Falls into place?

Falls to pieces is more like it.

His whole theory was built on ridiculous logic!

Forget built on, it was illogical from top to bottom—at the same time, though, our leader did set an example by boldly presenting his daydream of a theory without the slightest sign of embarrassment or shame.

You could also say he did us a favor by lowering the bar.

"Well, let's withhold judgment till we've all presented our theories—anyone mind if I go next?" the delinquent volunteered.

Normally, Sakiguchi would have been the one to save face for the leader with a smooth segue like that—but even if the councilman and the bossman were the fiercest of enemies outside the art room, inside it they had each other's backs.

I'm not saying I had a problem with the delinquent

going next, of course.

I was secretly hoping his argument overlapped with mine—because then I wouldn't have to present mine at all.

10. The Bossman's and Mr. Bare-Legs' Theories

"Sorry, guys, but compared to the president's theory, mine is just ordinary reasoning… I'm not good at this theoretical stuff, and creativity ain't my thing."

This preface lowered the bar even further than the leader's theory already had, and while I considered joking that it was only natural for a bad boy not to be good at stuff, I wanted to keep on enjoying the delicious tea he made for us, so I decided to keep my mouth shut.

I'll skip the death by poisoning, thank you very much.

No surprise that he wasn't cut out for theorizing, and I could also see how someone in the culinary world, where following recipes is the basic key to success, wouldn't be much for creativity. On the other hand, that made me genuinely curious to hear the solution he'd come up with to this art-world mystery.

"Yesterday someone proposed that maybe the artist had copied the classic masterpieces for practice, but that idea got shot down, right? Like, what a pointless exercise. Well, I agree—in fact, you'd pick up some weird habits practicing like that. It's like trying to cook without any seasoning or something."

More like cooking without the main ingredients.

This didn't go for all thirty-three paintings, but since most of the originals were centered around human figures, they could generally be considered the primary element.

Wasn't that like trying to cook a steak dinner without the steak? I mean, mashed potatoes and salad and whatever else are great, but you can't call them a steak dinner.

"Right. So if they're not copies, and they're not exercises—what if they're neither copies nor exercises?"

"?"

Huh?

Wasn't that a tautology?

"In other words, something new?" Mr. Bare-Legs asked.

Since he was doing a headstand (headsit?) on the sofa, he automatically looked like he was just messing around, but apparently he was taking a surprisingly serious stance on the inside.

I'm not sure what things were like in the past, but this mystery-solving competition was the most detective-like thing we'd done since I joined the club.

Mr. Bare-Legs had lived a tumultuous life with only his own two legs to rely on, which may have given him maturity beyond his years, but he still hadn't lost the childish heart that made him want to play games like these.

He was a devoted follower of the club's rules.

Be a boy, be a detective.

To say nothing of the beauty of his legs, reputed to have shamed every girl at Yubiwa Academy into wearing black stockings.

But what did he mean by "something new"?

"Kind of like a parody or a cover of an old song, but not quite? What I mean is, they derive from the famous paintings they're based on, but the finished product is something completely different."

"So they're meant as challenges to the originals?" I asked, implying that this stinking delinquent just stole the idea I discarded yesterday (reeling all the while at the dizzying awfulness of my own personality).

"No, nothing so critical or malicious…"

Not critical, not malicious, got it.

Then are we talking about… satire?

That's the delinquent's area of expertise, after all.

"Are you suggesting something along the lines of Gauguin painting his own *Sunflowers* under the influence of Van Gogh's? An elaboration on a theme?" Sakiguchi asked.

Although the councilman wasn't fully engaged, I guess he wasn't entirely ignoring our conversation either—but the delinquent just looked confused.

"Van Gogh? Gauguin? Sunflowers? Who're they?"

Not only did he not know who Van Gogh and Gauguin were, he apparently thought "Sunflowers" was a person's name—actually, I was impressed that he managed to cobble together a theory at all with that level of background knowledge.

But while the delinquent unfortunately didn't get Sakiguchi's analogy, for me it was quite enlightening— yes, you definitely could call an elaboration like that "something new."

The paintings might include a dash of critique or provocation—or satirical spirit, even—but at the very least, they weren't meant as practical jokes.

"I see, I see. That's quite an interesting idea, Michiru. Untrained as my mind is, I lack a detailed knowledge of the art world, but your theory does seem like something out of a mystery novel."

Indeed.

After all, the whole detective genre can be traced back to a single story by Edgar Allan Poe.

"Hmm? Edgar Allan Poe? Who might that be?"

Sotoin sounded puzzled.

I guess the club member apple doesn't fall far from the club president tree. But more importantly, the leader of the Pretty Boy Detective Club doesn't know the origin of Edogawa Rampo's pen name??

"Ah ha ha, well, speaking of Edogawa Rampo, imagine someone published a book called *The Pretty Boy in the Attic*. Just as a for-instance. That'd be nothing more than a heartfelt homage to an illustrious predecessor, not a joke taken too far. See?"

Mr. Bare-Legs was just summing up the point, but I'd have to disagree—that would definitely be a joke taken too far.

Anyhow, as promised, the delinquent's reasoning wasn't at all creative, and it probably wasn't interesting enough to earn Sotoin's praise. But rather than ordinary, I'd call it decently sensible—why was this guy a delinquent, anyway?

Needless to say, though, there was a flaw in his logic.

The same flaw as in Sotoin's creative, interesting, beautiful, totally off-target theory—if these thirty-three paintings were parodies or "cover songs," then it would be unnatural for the *Mona Lisa*, the ultimate masterpiece, not to be among them.

As unnatural as it would be for a list of the thirty-three best classic mystery stories to omit "The Murders in the Rue Morgue"—whether or not you like the story's twist is up to you, but its historical significance goes far beyond any question of individual taste.

"The top thirty-three classic mysteries, you say?

Personally, I don't think you could leave out *The Tragedy of Y*."

Well, that was kind of a random response from Sakiguchi—he really didn't seem to have his head in the game.

What was he keeping to himself?

As long as it wasn't a dilemma involving his first-grade fiancée, I wished he would hurry up and unburden himself to us...

"Okay, me next."

But it was Mr. Bare-Legs who volunteered.

Hadn't he noticed that Sakiguchi was acting weird? Or, knowing Mr. Bare-Legs, maybe he had noticed and was just enjoying the weirdness.

As it turned out, the guy whose personality was just as bad as mine (though in a different way) presented a very in-character theory.

"Since I'm the athletic type, *as you can see*, I wasn't able to come up with an artistic interpretation like the president or Michiru. So I decided to just work with what I could see with my own two eyes. Like, if I were the artist, why would I have painted these pictures?"

Why?

In other words, what was the artist's motivation?

According to the delinquent's theory, the answer was originality and innovation.

"What you could see with your own two eyes,

eh? Yes, I do believe that sort of observation could get us to the truth. Nothing is more important when solving a mystery," Sotoin announced with a satisfied nod, although it was unclear whether this nod reflected any real understanding of what Mr. Bare-Legs had in mind.

So, just to clarify, I dutifully asked, "What do you mean, Ashikaga?" Though it felt strange to call him that, since I'm so used to calling him Mr. Bare-Legs in my head.

And, though it probably had nothing to do with my straightforward question, he nonetheless gave a straightforward answer:

"Specifically, I thought if I were the artist, why wouldn't I just copy the paintings as is—like, if you had the skills, you'd want to make exact copies of those masterpieces, right? Without any unnecessary elaborations," he finished, adding his own unnecessary dig at the end.

The delinquent clicked his tongue softly at this, but Mr. Bare-Legs had pointed out another hole in his logic.

After all, the artist's innovation hadn't exactly improved the paintings.

It was perfectly fine as an artistic experiment, but I'd hardly call the results successful.

Looking at the thirty-three paintings, you didn't just think, "Hey, these are good." You thought, "Hey, these would be better if the artist had stuck to the originals."

Mr. Bare-Legs must have had the same thought, because he used that warped logic as the starting point to develop his argument.

"What on earth could make someone commit the grievous crime of removing the nudes from a bunch of nude paintings? I used that question as the starting point to develop my argument."

…Okay, so it was even more warped than I'd imagined, but at least he was consistent—and that's something, anyway.

And the conclusion was the same.

Just because I dress as a boy doesn't mean I have a special interest in naked women, but I did find it mysterious that someone would take the bathers out of *The Bathers*.

Mr. Bare-Legs explained the mystery like this:

"I figure maybe the artist was bad at painting people."

Well, that was blunt.

"Since people were a stumbling block, the artist just left them out of the paintings to make it easier. Seems to me that would explain all thirty-three of 'em."

So instead of painting an inferior nude, the artist thought it would be better to just leave that part up to the imagination? Well, I couldn't give Mr. Bare-Legs the vote of confidence he wanted, but as a layperson,

I could totally understand the practical, completely unartistic sentiment behind not painting what you're bad at painting.

And his theory did provide an explanation for why a painting based on the *Mona Lisa* wasn't among the collection.

The artist was no good at copying Leonardo's style, so he or she just didn't paint that one. No, not "didn't paint"—"couldn't paint."

Simple as that.

As for the inability to depict human beings, well, I believe that's a standard criticism of mystery novels as well…

I couldn't really imagine a more satisfying line of reasoning—but this one, too, had a hole. Or rather, a flaw.

And for a member of the Pretty Boy Detective Club, this flaw was fatal—his theory *wasn't beautiful.*

The very fact that it *made sense* to an ordinary person like me was already a problem.

But I hardly needed to point that out; Mr. Bare-Legs seemed well aware that his theory wasn't decisively convincing, because he promptly handed me the baton.

"Let's hear your theory, Doji!"

Dear oh dear, my turn had come.

It was time to shine.

Sadly, neither the delinquent's theory nor Mr. Bare-

Legs' overlapped with mine—so, reluctant as I was, it looked like I had no choice but to step up to the podium.

Though strictly speaking, the theory I was about to present wasn't even mine…

11. Mayumi Dojima's Theory?

"Okay, this is more a wild guess than a theory... I'm not really the artistically sensitive type, you know," I began.

Though I'm not the athletic type, either.

So what am I?

I wouldn't exactly call stargazing my specialty—I guess if I had to choose something, it would be eyesight?

Yes. Eyesight is my area of expertise.

"Ashikaga proposed that the artist gave up on drawing the people in the paintings because he or she wasn't any good at it, but I took things back a step and thought, what if the artist *couldn't see* the people—"

"Couldn't see the people? What the hell is that supposed to mean?"

The delinquent frowned.

He hadn't made a peep about the leader's theory, but apparently I didn't warrant the same kindness.

Of course, given how short on eloquence and confidence my presentation was, someone was bound to jump on it.

But now that I'd started, it was too late to stop.

"Look, eyesight isn't the same for everyone, right? I'm a perfect example. When I take off my glasses, the scene I see is totally different from what the delinquent sees—and if we both tried to paint that scene, we'd end up with two completely different pictures."

"First of all, stop calling me the delinquent. I just don't get it," the delinquent grumbled.

I'm sure he was referring to my theory, of course, and not my nickname for him.

I was hoping Sakiguchi would come to my rescue with a hearty "That's it!" but he had his head down in deep-thought mode—I know I'm a poor speaker compared to him, but I hoped he would at least listen!

"Um, let's see, they say mantis shrimp can see all kinds of wavelengths of light that humans can't see, right? And a spider perceives the world with eight eyes—and dragonflies have compound eyes."

"I'm getting more and more confused, and this shit about compound eyes is only compounding the problem. You saying a shrimp or a spider or a dragonfly painted those pictures?"

The delinquent sounded like he was trying to pick a fight, but at least he was sinking his teeth into my presentation, which I guess made sense for a chef who didn't turn up his nose at anything—instead of Michiru the

Epicure, maybe we should call him Michiru the Epic Glutton.

"But young Dojima, isn't the notion that the artist wasn't human simply too fantastic?" asked Sotoin. That's right, Sotoin was questioning my rationality.

But that's not what I was saying.

If I had that much imagination, my life wouldn't be the way it is.

"All I'm trying to say is that eyesight isn't uniform. I didn't mean the artist was a shrimp or a spider or a dragonfly—never mind all that, even if we're just talking about human beings, not everyone's vision is the same…"

I was back where I'd started.

This wasn't working, time to change tack.

Let me see… How had *he* put it?

"Okay, take rainbows. We typically say rainbows have seven colors, but that's not necessarily true. Some people see ten or twelve colors, and others only see five or even three—some people have trouble distinguishing between green and blue, while others can divide green into dozens of shades. And some people think pink is the same as rose."

"You mean like how blackboards are actually green?"

Mr. Bare-Legs' response was vigorously far removed from my metaphor, but I suppose the basic point was the same—after all, if a very dark green looks black to you, then black it is.

"Ashikaga said earlier that he'd decided to work with what he could see with his own two eyes, but everyone's eyes see something different, so everyone will paint something different—you could even say that's how art can exist in the first place. If we take that to its logical extreme, looking at masterpieces of the past is kind of like seeing the world through the eyes of a genius—"

I realized they were all giving me strange looks.

Crap, I'd stunned them by saying something out of character—which made sense, considering I hadn't come up with those lines in the first place.

Their amazement was itself very much based on something.

The person giving me the strangest look of all was Sakiguchi, who hadn't even seemed to be listening—but of course, he was like a bloodhound when he caught even a whiff of his sworn enemy.

I had to get back on track, no matter how haphazardly.

"Anyway, my theory is that the artist intended to copy the old masters for practice or whatever, but the end result turned out totally different."

"…So you're saying the artist had vision like yours, and unintentionally saw right through the people in the paintings?"

Ah.

That was a much clearer way of putting it.

"Amazing! Those simple mental circuits of yours sure do the job!"

"I'm overjoyed you finally feel comfortable enough around us to open up," the delinquent said with a shrug, before adding, "but I'm not so sure about your theory. First off, I doubt many people have eyesight like yours, kid… And even if they did, they'd be seeing through some paint on a canvas, not a real person, right? So even if they saw through the paint, all they'd see would be a blank canvas. It's not like the backgrounds would be painted in behind the human figures in the originals."

Looks like the delinquent's mental circuits weren't quite as simple as I'd thought—his points were all on point.

Well, it's not like I was genuinely saying that the masterpieces looked this or that way to the artist—I knew better than anyone that every person sees the world differently, both functionally and metaphorically, but I didn't think the theory I'd just presented was particularly realistic.

I was just parroting most of it anyway.

I'd been curious to see how everyone would react to the idea, that's all.

"How do you explain the fact that the *Mona Lisa* isn't included?" Mr. Bare-Legs asked.

"With the *Mona Lisa*, I think the artist might have seen through the whole thing, not just the human subject," I answered.

This was a pretty broad interpretation of my theory, so much so that if we accepted that, it felt like anything could go, but nevertheless, it did explain the omission.

Broad interpretation or no, a theory was a theory.

"Hmm. That sounds more like the sophistry of a criminal than a theory to me," Sakiguchi declared. His voice was gentle, but his point was harsh—at first I thought he was praising me because of that beautiful voice, but no, however broadly I interpreted his comment, he was definitely insinuating something. He himself looked unsure why he'd chosen such sharp words, but I had a pretty good guess, so it didn't really hurt my feelings.

The sophistry of a criminal.

Right on the money.

"Not half bad for your first attempt at deduction, young Dojima! Sophistry it may be, but what graceful, beautiful sophistry!"

This comment from our leader, who's always one for positive reinforcement, brought my presentation to an end—which meant it was finally time for Sakiguchi's eagerly awaited contribution.

Or at least that's what I assumed, but I was wrong.

"Next let's hear from Sosaku!"

12. The Child Genius's Theory

Huh? Yubiwa was presenting a theory?

He's so taciturn that I assumed he'd stick to the role of audience at this little gathering—but now he was about to bust out an eloquent speech?

I was suddenly on the edge of my seat, but my hopes were dashed a moment later—because he just muttered, "That's not all of them."

A mere five words.

Then he added, "There are thirty-three more, at least."

"What? What do you mean?" I asked reflexively, but he'd already returned to his usual silent self—it appeared no further explanation would be forthcoming.

I looked in turn at the delinquent, Mr. Bare-Legs, and Sakiguchi to see if they'd understood, but they looked even more confused than they'd been during my own bonkers presentation—Sotoin was the only exception.

"Aha! So that's it!" he cried, slapping his knee,

although I seriously questioned the depth of his comprehension.

But one must never doubt one's leader.

Reassuring myself that he alone must have caught the gist of the child genius's theory, I asked him for an explanation.

At least Sotoin seemed to have some telepathic ability, which was better than the child genius's steadfast silence.

"Dear me, young Dojima, you didn't understand? Sosaku said, 'That's not all of them. There are thirty-three more, at least.'"

"Right, right. And?"

"And? And that's all…"

That's all?

Speaking up had only set me back.

But judging by what the loyal Sakiguchi said next, the leader's words were gospel even when he was simply passing along a message from the child genius.

"Indeed, there is no reason to believe the set of paintings we discovered is complete. You couldn't be more right."

A little too loyal to elementary school students.

Or was his mind still miles away?

"If, as Sosaku suggests, there are another thirty-three paintings in this series, then those missing canvases might include Leonardo's *Mona Lisa* and Munch's *The*

Scream."

"But those were the only canvases in the crawl space, Mr. Vice Squad … I mean, Vice President."

"I can't believe that was an innocent slip of the tongue."

I thought I could get away with it because he was spacing out, but apparently he wasn't *that* spaced out.

"Anyway, you're right. But who's to say the crawl space was the artist's only hiding spot?"

"Good point. Dojima'll just have to poke around in all the crawl spaces in the school …" the delinquent said, stroking his chin—although I'm pretty sure it was just to hide his grin, not because he was lost in thought.

What the hell was he suggesting?

If the leader latched onto that idea, I'd be screwed.

"They don't necessarily have to be hidden in a crawl space, though!" I added hastily. "I mean, they could be under the floor!"

"You'd be doing pretty much the same thing either way, considering how the school's put together," the delinquent retorted.

Which was true.

"I can see how there might be more paintings, but Yubiwa, how did you come up with 'at least thirty-three more'? Isn't that a little too specific?"

Just as I expected, he completely ignored my question.

what a master speaker he was.

Or so I thought, but his long face didn't exactly shout, "I'm raring to go!"

"Ah, well. It's my turn already? Where shall I begin, I wonder—yes, that will do. To make a long story short, I have succeeded in confirming the identity of the person who painted the pictures we discovered in the crawl space."

If I'd been sipping a cup of tea at that moment, even one specially blended to suit my tastes, I would have sprayed it all over the place—that's how explosive this revelation was.

He'd identified the artist?

Wasn't that the same as solving the mystery?

He'd said it so casually, but he might as well have topped it off with a Q. E. D.!

His long face hadn't lost its gloomy tinge, though—not at all the air of a great detective who had just discovered the truth.

"The artist's name is Kowako Towai. She used to be an art teacher at this school."

13. Kowako Towai

An art teacher.

The answer had been in a sort of blind spot, but once he said it, I felt it'd been staring us in the face all along—it should have been my very next thought after I proposed that the paintings might be student projects.

Since they had been hidden in the crawl space above the art room, it was only natural to assume that whoever painted them had some kind of *connection* to the art room.

In which case it was only natural to assume that directing one's inquiries to the school, as Sakiguchi had done, would uncover the artist's identity.

But if that was true, why had we even bothered with this war of words, or rather, brainstorming session? Our wannabe version of the Black Widowers felt downright pointless.

Speaking of which, the Black Widowers may not have been a boy's detective club, but it *was* no-girls-

allowed, if I remember correctly… Somewhat distracted by this relatively irrelevant thought, I gave an internal
nod of satisfaction as I grasped the likely reason for Sakiguchi's gloomy mood.

To put it bluntly, given that he'd actually *solved the
mystery*, I could see how he'd have a hard time introducing his excessively realistic theory into this contest where
beauty came before truth, and the ruling principle was
the more fantastical the theory, the higher the praise.

I could well imagine how he must have felt as he
listened to each of us present our theories—no wonder
he'd been tuning it out.

Or so I thought, but apparently such concerns didn't
explain his mood, because he seemed just as tense and
unhappy after presenting his "solution" in that beautiful
voice of his as he had before.

What was going on?

"Look, kid. Just because he figured out who painted
the pictures doesn't mean he figured out *why* she painted
them—the mystery isn't solved yet."

"Sure, but if he asked around in the teachers'
lounge—"

No.

Sakiguchi had said "used to."

Kowako Towai "used to be an art teacher at this
school"—which suggested she wasn't anymore.

I've said it a million times:

Electives were eliminated from Yubiwa Academy's curriculum ages ago—which is why this room wasn't being used, which is why a crew of weirdos called the Pretty Boy Detective Club had been able to commandeer it.

"Hey, so like, when you say 'used to,' how long ago do you mean?" Mr. Bare-Legs asked.

"Seven years ago," Sakiguchi replied curtly—like his mind was on something else.

He seemed distracted by the question of how to continue with the meat of his presentation, which was still to come.

"Seven years ago, huh? So, back when your fiancée was just a twinkle in her daddy's eye, then."

"That is correct, but was such a comment necessary at this juncture?"

His mind might be elsewhere, but he could still manage a sharp retort—wait, his fiancée wasn't even seven yet?

I suddenly wished we could get to work on that particular problem instead...

"So she was the artist, huh?" Mr. Bare-Legs went on. "But, Nagahiro's the oldest, and he hasn't even met this teacher, so obviously neither have I—doesn't really tell us much, does it? I mean, we don't even have any idea what kind of person this lady is."

Well, we knew she was the kind of lady who would remove the people from famous paintings—and while the quality of her work suggested she must have been competent as an art teacher and an artist, she was also unquestionably an oddball.

Still, being a second-year myself, I obviously hadn't known her either—never mind Sotoin, who wasn't all that much older than seven himself.

"Interesting! So in other words, when they dropped art from the curriculum seven years ago, they let Ms. Towai go as well!" Sotoin exclaimed cheerfully.

For once his insight was a good one, though personally I try not to talk about grownups losing their jobs in such a jolly tone.

"So you think she stuffed the paintings up in the crawl space when she got fired?"

I kept the hole in the ceiling in sight as I added my own insight.

It's possible we never would've noticed the removable panel if we hadn't decided to paint a mural on the ceiling, but it made sense that the former occupant of this room—the art teacher—would've known about it. Though it was also conceivable that Ms. Towai had rigged it up herself.

She hadn't known what to do with all those canvases when she left the school, so she'd hidden them up there where they'd be out of sight—hardly the praiseworthy act of a sensible adult, but plausible nonetheless.

All the more plausible if she was getting them back

for firing her—although that could hardly be called a beautiful solution to our mystery.

"Um, Sakiguchi, I can see how finding out about that teacher would have been easy enough, but how did you know she was the artist? Sure, the art teacher would be a prime suspect since the paintings were in the art room crawl space, but that's not exactly proof, is it?"

There was no getting around the fact that the thirty-three paintings were unsigned—and not even initialed.

The simple fact that Ms. Towai was the art teacher wasn't conclusive evidence that she'd painted them.

"You're right, I don't even have circumstantial evidence—all I have is hearsay."

"Hearsay?"

"Just what I gathered from asking around with some teachers I know from the student council…"

What was going on here?

That was one hell of a vague answer, coming from Nagahiro the Orator.

Or was it the answer from "some teachers" that had been vague?

Which was reasonable, given that this all happened seven years ago.

But why did Sakiguchi think he could determine the identity of the artist based on such vague evidence? Had Ms. Towai been so legendary that teachers were still talking about her seven years after her departure?

"Yes, she does seem to have been quite the celebrity."

Everything Sakiguchi was saying boiled down to hearsay, not clear-cut fact—despite the crystal-clear voice he was saying it in. Still, Kowako Towai... It was a distinctive name, and I felt as if I'd heard it somewhere before.

She was long gone by the time I arrived at Yubiwa Middle, so if her name sounded familiar, I must have heard it outside of school—maybe I knew her as an artist, rather than a teacher?

"I doubt it, Dojima. Forget 'sounded familiar,' try 'looked familiar'—I thought I recognized the name Towai, too, but it's from inside the school, not outside of it," the delinquent said. "You know that humongous painting in the auditorium? Wasn't Kowako Towai the name of the person who painted it?"

It came to me in a flash.

Yubiwa Academy prided itself on the auditorium where all its gatherings took place, from ceremonies at the start and end of each year to Monday morning assemblies, all-school events, entrance ceremonies, and graduations.

And just as the delinquent said, a huge painting adorned the wall of that auditorium.

I couldn't picture it exactly, but I seemed to recall a plaque underneath it which gave the title of the painting and the name of the artist—and if we could trust the delinquent's memory, that name was Kowako Towai.

"Though I'm surprised a delinquent like you even knows the auditorium exists…"

"Want another cup of tea, Dojima?"

Just as the delinquent was plotting my death by poisoning, Sakiguchi stepped in.

"The auditorium, you say…" he murmured, nodding as he stood up from the sofa. "It seems Ms. Towai must've painted that picture while she was working here—well then. Shall we continue this conversation in front of the painting in question?"

14. The Auditorium in the Auditorium

"So this is a painting! I always thought it was wallpaper."

As Mr. Bare-Legs' comment vividly conveys, the painting was enormous—a layperson like me has no place even taking a stab at it, but the canvas must have been at least a size 1,000, maybe even 2,000.

Its presence was so overwhelming that it paradoxically melted into the background.

Actually, I'd never paid much attention to it during assemblies.

Look, a painting. That was about it.

But when I actually gave it a good look, I realized that even aside from the size, it was pretty strange.

Not in the same way as the thirty-three paintings in the art room; it wasn't like something was missing—it was weirder in a more concrete way.

Right below the painting was an inconspicuous plaque that did indeed name "Kowako Towai" as the artist. Above that was the title, which reflected the strangeness of the painting admirably.

The Auditorium in the Auditorium.

Just as the title suggested, it was a painting of an auditorium—*this* auditorium.

Not the outside, either, but the inside where we all stood—it was like a matryoshka doll, or two mirrors facing each other.

Needless to say, there was a huge painting of an auditorium on the wall of the auditorium in the painting—and while the next iteration wasn't as crisp, it went on like that ad infinitum.

"The auditorium in the auditorium in the auditorium in the auditorium in the auditorium in the auditorium in the auditorium in the auditorium in the auditorium..." Sotoin muttered, craning his neck up at the sprawling canvas—like he was naïvely enjoying himself.

Us middle school students were all sick of looking at it, but I guess an elementary kid seeing it for the first time would find it novel.

Ms. Towai had painted this picture.

Although the ratio of height to width was different, I think the dimensions were more or less on the same scale as the ceiling mural the child genius was working on—which made me curious to know what he thought of it, but his face as he stood looking up at the painting alongside the leader was unreadable.

"It's so damn huge, 'whoa' comes to mind before

anything like 'it's good.'"

This was the delinquent's take.

I doubt he came up with it on the spot. He'd probably been thinking the same thing for a long time—and true enough, painting something this big would definitely require skill in its own right.

But unlike the thirty-three canvases from the crawl space, this one (because it *was* one painting, no matter how big) surely wasn't based on a famous masterpiece.

After all, there was no way some illustrious artist whose name now graced the pages of history had stopped by Yubiwa Academy to paint a picture of its auditorium—the school wasn't that old to begin with, and even if it were, the brushwork on this painting seemed to have nothing in common with the set of thirty-three smaller canvases.

"That reminds me, Sotoin, you said you saw a similarity between the thirty-three paintings in the art room. Do you see the same thing in *The Auditorium in the Auditorium*?" I asked.

"Huh? Did I say that? When? Where? How many times has the Earth spun since then?"

I might as well have been speaking another language.

He acted so confused that I started to think I must've been mistaken, but no. He definitely said that. It was part of the foundation our whole theoretical exercise had been based on!

You can't just flip the script on us like that.

Now our only option was to rely on Sakiguchi.

Our student council president, Nagahiro Sakiguchi.

He still hadn't explained how he felt able to conclude that Kowako Towai had painted the thirty-three pictures.

"Not conclude. I can only conjecture, based on hearsay, that the likelihood is very high."

"Quit grandstanding, Nagahiro. Conjecture? Earlier you said you'd *confirmed* it. I don't know what you're waffling about, but keep up this mealy-mouthed crap and before you know it, your fiancée will be all grown up."

"Hyota, please don't mock me. And for the record, nothing would please me more than for my fiancée, who was chosen by my parents without my consent, to be all grown up."

Meeee neither.

Anyway, Hyota's prodding seemed to have firmed up the councilman's resolve.

"Ladies and gentlemen," he began—in a beautiful voice.

15. A Crime Proclaimed

"Ladies and gentlemen.

"My sincerest apologies for my earlier reticence. As your vice president, it is inexcusable for me to abandon the loquaciousness that is my one saving grace.

"No, Hyota, my elementary-school fiancée is *not* my second saving grace. I've finally made up my mind to speak, so I would appreciate if you didn't interrupt.

"Yes, the fact is, I did consider keeping this matter quietly to myself.

"As student council president of Yubiwa Academy, I couldn't help but wonder if it was wrong to dig into our school's shameful past.

"Yet since the whole business stemmed from the creation of a mural with which I was involved not as Nagahiro Sakiguchi, student council president, but as Nagahiro the Orator, vice president of the Pretty Boy Detective Club, I couldn't very well just clam up.

"Therefore, I solemnly present you with the results

of my investigation.

"Of course, the teachers I questioned were even more reticent than I—were I to repeat to you verbatim what they told me, without some measure of editorial intervention, you would surely be frustrated beyond measure. Hyota might even be bored enough to leave.

"Which is to say, the art teacher in question, Kowako Towai, was abundantly capable of inspiring reticence.

"She was such a legendary teacher that she is still spoken of in the teachers' lounge seven years after her departure, but the legend is by no means a positive one.

"Our teachers are adults, and all of this took place long ago, so they did not malign or openly disparage her—they were reticent, as I've said—yet they could still not fully conceal the extent of Ms. Towai's odd behavior.

"To put it bluntly, she was an oddball.

"That may be quite appropriate for an artist, but to be frank, the artist in question was apparently a problem teacher.

"Of course, the reason she resigned… Or, let's not mince words, the reason she was fired, was the elimination of art electives from Yubiwa Academy's curriculum. But that was partially a pretext.

"It's quite ironic, of course, for a teacher to demonstrate to her students through the arc of her own career that your past behavior catches up with you in the end.

"To give just a few examples of her eccentricity:

"She held a sketching competition without school permission, and took an entire class overseas to participate.

"She remodeled the school willy-nilly, installing doors to nowhere in some places and removing doors and windows in others; she constructed meaningless secret rooms, and turned straight hallways into winding mazes.

"She acted as nude model for her own classes, although that was one of her more endearing episodes.

"Hyota, please control your reaction to the simple phrase 'nude model.' Perhaps you'll cool down if I relate the anecdote about her instructing the female students to draw the boys on the swim team in their swimsuits.

"She appears to have believed that art and nudity could not be separated—but that doesn't change the fact that she clearly went too far.

"Whether seven years ago or seventy, her behavior was just as unacceptable as it would be today.

"It would be all over the headlines, no question.

"The school seems to have adroitly covered it all up, but in any case, Ms. Towai appears to have been something of an anarchic presence.

"Even if art classes hadn't been eliminated seven years ago, I'm sure this exceptional woman would have been pressured to resign sooner or later.

"She was an antisocial element, and it would come as no surprise if she had even been arrested—but at the risk of repeating myself, as an artist she seems to have been quite well respected.

"She had the standing to be called *sensei* in the art world as well as at school—in fact, her artistic achievements are what earned her an invitation to teach at Yubiwa Academy in the first place.

"The punchline, however, was that the talent scout who recruited her subsequently had a nervous breakdown—Kowako Towai seems to have been well known as a demonic presence in the contemporary art world going back to her teens.

"This enormous painting was apparently her first undertaking after coming to the school—and I think you will agree it gives a clear sense of her unusual character.

"She commandeered the auditorium for a full month in order to paint it, and so from the time of her arrival she was already something of a legend.

"No, I myself had not heard of her before I began this investigation. She may have been well known in the world of contemporary art, but as you might guess, she wasn't the type to give interviews. Accordingly, she was virtually unknown to the general populace—a rising star of the art world known only to the select few.

"A rising star, or rather…

"When she was our age, she was known as the Black

Hole—no, Michiru.

"I have not jumped to the conclusion that the paintings hidden in the crawl space were painted by Kowako Towai merely because she was such an eccentric—though needless to say, she seems to have been capable of anything, and she did do whatever she wanted with that art room.

"What was that, Ms. Dojima?

"You have a comment regarding my statement that she did whatever she wanted with the art room…? Well, let us continue.

"At the very least, installing an entrance to the crawl space seems entirely in line with her behavior.

"However, she does not appear to have had the tendencies Hyota and Ms. Dojima have proposed.

"I don't believe she avoided painting the human form because she was bad at it, or that she saw through the people in famous paintings.

"To the contrary, I believe she painted exactly what she wanted to paint, with no such limitations.

"She seems to have had quite the eye for art, as well.

"Yes, leaving aside the question of her teaching, she was a top-flight artist—each of us is cut out for some things more than others.

"So if I were to evaluate the theories presented thus far, I would say that Michiru's likely hews closest to the truth.

"…Ms. Dojima, I see no cause for that expression. Just how much do you look down on Michiru, anyway?

"Of course, this is all assuming that Kowako Towai was indeed the artist—so I will now explain my reasons for that assumption.

"It happened seven years ago.

"Precisely as the electives—and art, in particular—disappeared from the curriculum.

"Let us consider their removal a sign of the times, and for the moment leave aside the question of its wisdom.

"A decision was made to move in that direction, in accordance with school policy—and I hesitate to condemn it, because after all, if art class had not been eliminated, we would not be using the art room as our headquarters today.

"However.

"Ms. Towai opposed the decision with all her might.

"That surprises you? Well, the school was surprised, too, it seems—since from what I've heard, she didn't seem to think of herself as a teacher, not one bit.

"Because she had a certain standing as an artist and received fanatical rave reviews in the art world, if nowhere else, no one dreamed she would put up a fight when they tried to fire her from the school.

"Well, even if the decision was natural enough, it was also somewhat high-handed—first the school invites her to teach, then they put her out to pasture the moment it suits them. Anyone would be angry.

"But Kowako Towai was not just anyone.

"Such reasonable grievances were not why she put up a fight—never mind that it should have been the perfect opportunity for her to step away from teaching duties which had nothing to do with her creative pursuits.

"*She said the children needed art.*

"She dug in her heels.

"…Though apparently there was a great deal of doubt about how genuine her sentiment really was. Her past behavior had been so appalling that no one believed anything she said.

"Michiru, please take this to heart. When push comes to shove, it's how you behave the rest of the time that counts.

"All the gossips whispered that she was simply fishing for a bigger severance package… Making art is expensive, after all.

"The fact is, however, she had been offered an enormous severance package from the start, and yet she couldn't have cared less about it.

"No matter how they tried to placate or cajole her, she wouldn't budge. She continued to resist, alone—and in the end, she grew almost threatening.

"Yes, threatening.

"Or rather, she made what seemed to be an actual

threat.

"'Children should not be in a school where art is not taught—so if you insist on implementing your decision…'

"'*I will kidnap every student in this school.*'

"That is what she apparently said.

"Or rather.

"That is how she proclaimed her intended crime."

16. A Kidnapping Carried Out

"K-Kidnap every student?" I repeated.

I thought that maybe echoing Sakiguchi's words would help me understand them, but no, they remained beyond all comprehension.

I mean, even seven years ago, Yubiwa Academy was probably mammoth.

With all this doom and gloom about the decreasing birth rate in Japan, it stands to reason that there would've been even more kids seven years ago than there are now—and even if her words were just tit for tat, kidnapping *all* the students? There's such a thing as laying it on *too* thick.

"Reminds me of, whatchamacallit, that guy who played the flute," the delinquent said, displaying just how shallow his knowledge really was.

Gimme a… This ignoramus's theory is the current front-runner?

Which reminded me, earlier Sakiguchi had offhandedly praised the leader's theory, but now he wasn't commenting on it at all (he'll go far, mark my words). Logically, though, if Ms. Towai was the artist, the thirty-three paintings couldn't possibly have been the antecedents of historical masterpieces.

Not that Sotoin's preposterous theory even merited serious discussion, but... Fortunately, the president didn't seem to care about it (or the fact that he himself had proposed it) at all.

He was too riveted by the story of the strange artist who once taught at our school—he looked as if he could barely contain his excitement as he listened to his subordinate's report.

Maybe he identified with Towai's eccentricity, as Sakiguchi described it—maybe he sensed a certain aesthetic in it.

As a member of the Pretty Boy Detective Club, I couldn't very well disagree with her insistence that "children need art" either, although I'm sure I can only say that because I wasn't around to see it for myself.

...Oh, and to give a belated interpretation of the delinquent's vague comment, I'm pretty sure he was talking about *The Pied Piper of Hamelin*.

That tale is about music rather than painting, but they're both creative arts, so close enough—anyway, it's the story of a man who kidnapped all the children in a certain village by playing on his flute.

I've heard it's based on a true story, too… But, was Sakiguchi saying that this teacher had announced she would carry out a similar mass kidnapping?

Just like an artist.

Artists always seem to be making overblown claims like that—but if she was just trying to get in the last word as the grand finale to her solitary resistance movement, it smelled a bit like sour grapes.

It was an impossible boast to make good on.

It didn't even constitute a threat.

Probably all she got were a few contemptuous laughs—or so I thought, but Sakiguchi shook his head.

"Ms. Towai carried out her threat."

She kidnapped all the students.

His voice grave, Sakiguchi turned to the wall of the auditorium.

The wall with the enormous painting on it.

The Auditorium in the Auditorium.

By Kowako Towai.

So? Why was he focusing on the painting right now?

Why had he asked us to come to the auditorium while he told Ms. Towai's story? If he was only planning to describe her strange behavior, couldn't we just have stayed in the art room?

The Pretty Boy Detective Club operated in secret (no doubt because secrecy was beautiful according to the club's aesthetic), and its members normally avoided doing anything that would draw attention to themselves outside the art room.

At the moment no one else was in the auditorium, but if the councilman and the bossman were spotted together, it'd make the front page of the school paper tomorrow—though I'm not sure we even have a school paper.

"You see, originally," Sakiguchi began, as if in direct answer to my lingering questions, "this painting depicted a meeting of the entire student body of Yubiwa Academy Middle School—but seven years ago, Ms. Towai kidnapped them, *leaving not a single one of the painted students behind.*"

The painted auditorium was empty.

As empty as the real auditorium was right now, just before the end of the school day.

Not a single student remained.

17. Mass Kidnapping from a Massive Painting

Interesting—so that was his evidence.

In other words, Ms. Towai had a "criminal record" dating back to when she left Yubiwa Academy seven years ago—she had "kidnapped" the people from a painting.

Of course, there were some differences between the two cases.

There was the scale, for one, and the fact that in the case of this mass kidnapping, she'd removed the people from her own painting, not from masterworks of the past.

Also, calling it a kidnapping was never anything but a metaphor—since she must've just replaced the painting that showed the entire student body attending an assembly with one of an empty auditorium, after all the students had left.

There were things about it that still didn't quite add up, but in contrast to the other eccentricities Sakiguchi had told us about, this act seemed designed to carry a powerful message.

Though I'm not sure whether she meant to imply that the students would desert a school that treated art so cavalierly, or something else entirely.

Anyway.

She had followed through on her threat.

"You ask me, she didn't just send a message, she messed with the law. She may have painted that picture, but the school owned it, and she switched it without permission. That's a hell of a lot different than fiddling around with some old paintings," the delinquent commented.

Not a surprise that he knows so much about breaking the law.

"Are you saying that was the real reason she got fired?" Mr. Bare-Legs asked.

"No," Sakiguchi replied. "Strictly speaking, no one ever proved it was Ms. Towai who switched the paintings. By the time the switch was discovered, she'd gone missing."

"Gone missing?"

"Yes. Her resignation was found lying in front of the new painting like she'd slammed it down there before she left... But she never claimed her severance package, and she disappeared without a trace." Sakiguchi shook his head. "To this day, no one knows what became of her."

After "disappearing" the entire student body from the painting, the artist herself had "disappeared"—how bizarre.

"So when she quit teaching, she quit painting, too?"

"It appears so—she ceased all public activities, and even the fact of her disappearance isn't widely known."

In other words, there was no direct evidence that Ms. Towai was responsible for the switch, which was itself the basis of our circumstantial evidence that she was responsible for the thirty-three paintings in the art room? Maybe she was using her own disappearance to shift the blame for the crime.

But given the circumstances, it was hard to come up with any other likely suspect—even if she hadn't announced her crime in advance, who else would derive any meaning from changing one painting for another?

"It's hard to imagine it was meaningful for her, either," Mr. Bare-Legs said. "It's not like the school kept art in the curriculum because of what she did, right?"

"Correct. On the contrary—Ms. Towai's disappearance became an opportunity for the school to eliminate electives completely," Sakiguchi replied.

"Truly meaningless," our leader said with a nod. "But that is exactly what makes it beautiful! Kidnapping an entire school without harming anyone or even really causing them any trouble is no easy feat."

I guess his sympathies really did lie with the artist.

It made sense that Manabu the Aesthete didn't simply pity the art teacher but genuinely sympathized with her—but then, you'd think Manabu the Aesthete wouldn't be the one whose sympathies were strongest.

What about Sosaku the Artiste?

I looked over at the child genius.

He'd been listening to Sakiguchi's explanation so quietly I'd forgotten he was even there—what could be going through his mind?

As usual, I couldn't tell a thing from his perfectly blank expression.

There was no way he was indifferent to it, though, both as a member of the Pretty Boy Detective Club and as an artist.

Plus.

He was heir to the Yubiwa Foundation, the parent organization of Yubiwa Academy—in other words, the guy who would one day take over the organization that had fired Ms. Towai.

He wasn't responsible for that, of course, but perhaps he felt some kind of connection to the whole episode?

"But Mr. President, people *were* harmed, weren't they? It *did* cause them trouble. We've been calling what she did 'switching' the paintings, but we coulda called it theft," the delinquent pointed out, pragmatically enough.

Hmm, I suppose he was right.

"Don't you think maybe she split because if the school filed a police report, she coulda been arrested, not just fired? 'Course, from what Nagahiro says, it sounds like they hushed it all up."

"Hushed it up—indeed. Well, I presume the school was wary of too much publicity, given how hard they had pushed the changes to the curriculum. Yubiwa Academy isn't the first school to keep things to itself, you know. Educational institutions have always been insular."

Sakiguchi probably added that last bit for the child genius's benefit—though in my opinion even the most secretive organization would be likely to tell the police about a theft that massive.

Had they decided that an artist stealing her own work didn't constitute a crime?

"Naturally that was part of it—but the main reason Yubiwa Academy didn't file a police report was that the mass kidnapping in question was an impossible crime."

"An impossible crime? Um… Isn't that a bit of an overstatement?" I couldn't help asking.

If she'd genuinely kidnapped every student in the school, that would have been the very definition of an impossible crime, but the fact was that all Ms. Towai had done was switch one painting for another—wait a minute, all?

All she'd done?

This painting?

This humongous, size 1,000 or even 2,000 painting?

I finally realized why Sakiguchi had been acting so glum—it had nothing to do with uncovering the shameful past of our school.

He thought he was solving the mystery, but instead, he'd found *a new mystery*—which was precisely the opposite of detective work.

Nevertheless, I kept pressing him.

"Sakiguchi."

I couldn't help myself.

"How did Ms. Towai switch a pair of paintings— *that are way bigger than the entrance to the auditorium*?"

18. Ship in a Bottle

Think of a ship in a bottle.

The only way a ship bigger than the mouth of the bottle could get in there is for someone to stick the pieces of the ship in one by one, then assemble them with a pair of tweezers—just like Ms. Towai must have done when she painted *The Auditorium in the Auditorium*.

She must've brought the materials in separately, then stretched the canvas right there in the auditorium before beginning work on her enormous painting—but she couldn't have used the same method for the switch-up.

Because whatever artistic message she may have been sending, her actions did have a criminal aspect to them, so she couldn't have afforded any witnesses.

Both lugging in an unstretched canvas and painting the second painting inside the auditorium would have been out of the question—someone from the school definitely would have caught her in the act.

I mean, the painting was so huge that when she was first hired, she'd had to take over the auditorium for a whole month to finish it—if she wanted to switch it out, her only option would have been to paint the replacement somewhere else and bring it in once it was done. But the completed painting was far, far too big to fit through the auditorium door, which meant she couldn't have brought it in after it was finished.

It was impossible.

An impossible crime.

A locked-room mystery, albeit an unorthodox one—I could see how the officials at Yubiwa Academy would've been reluctant to report it to the police.

"Okay, but come on. It's not like she actually kidnapped the entire student body from inside the picture," the delinquent said.

But maybe the school officials did consider it a possibility.

That might be why this painting still hung in its original spot seven years later—otherwise, I can't imagine why the school would leave up a painting by some problem teacher.

They were leaving a place for the kidnapped students *to return to*—or even if they weren't quite that sentimental, I bet they just felt it was too creepy to get rid of.

Which was reasonable.

I mean, it even creeped me out.

I shivered at the thought that I'd been absentmindedly looking up at it for more than a year and a half, ever since I first set foot in the auditorium during my entrance ceremony—though of course I wasn't about to swallow some absurd story about students being kidnapped from a picture.

However.

One person had swallowed it wholesale.

"Beautiful!"

Sotoin clapped boisterously, then reached out to shake Sakiguchi's hand.

"Excellent work, Nagahiro! You had good reason for grandstanding! That beautiful hidden ball trick you just performed is further proof that I was not mistaken in appointing you vice president! It was so dazzling, in fact, that I can't help but think you're after my position as president!"

"Ha…ha ha, what are you saying, Mr. President? To think that I would have designs on your position… I-It's unimaginable. Quite out of the question."

Why was he so shaken?

All the same, Sotoin's praise did appear to finally relax him.

The leader seemed to view the discovery of a new mystery as cause for celebration—he was a "detective," of a sort anyway, so you'd think his greatest joy would lie in solving mysteries, but apparently nothing could beat having more of them to solve, so long as they were beautiful.

If you asked me, though, the situation seemed to be getting more puzzling by the minute—because if the canvases we'd found really were painted by this problem teacher Kowako Towai, then all of our theories had missed the mark.

The delinquent's idea may have been the best we had at the moment, but there was no guarantee he was right.

Neither was there anything in Ms. Towai's story to back up the theory presented by the child genius (or more accurately, by his spokesman Sotoin) that there were at least another thirty-three paintings (Sakiguchi's silence on the subject spoke to his thorough discretion toward those with power and influence).

"The easiest way to sort this all out would've been to just ask Ms. Towai, but if she's gone missing, guess there's not much we can do. Missing, like the people in the paintings… Kinda sounds like it means something, but I'm not sure what…"

Mr. Bare-Legs seemed as lost as I was—as a jock, art was outside his field of expertise (nudes aside), so once things got this tangled up, I guess he felt helpless.

I hardly need mention the delinquent's reaction.

The leader, however, seemed suddenly energized.

"As detectives, it would not be fitting for us to ask the artist to explain her own actions! In my opinion, the confession of a criminal does not constitute evidence!" he proclaimed with great enthusiasm.

Never mind that what he said made no sense whatsoever.

Although I suppose it was preferable to pinning your entire investigation on eliciting a confession—which detectives in mystery novels do as a matter of course. But if you really think about it, that's a pretty scary thing to do.

Anyway, the leader being who he is, he generously conceded, "I would of course be happy to speak with Madame Towai if we were merely confirming the accuracy of our own solution. Nagahiro, knowing you, I have no doubt that even if you haven't yet located Madame Towai, you are already investigating her whereabouts. How soon can you find her?"

"It's difficult to say… I am indeed in the midst of an inquiry into the matter, but it's rather like trying to catch a cloud—at present I don't even know if she is still alive."

She wasn't just missing, she was MIA.

A bona fide seven-year disappearance.

Even if she were still alive, that was long enough to have her declared officially dead by filing a missing persons report—and no matter how much support Sakiguchi enjoyed as president of the student council, searching for a missing person off campus couldn't be all that easy.

And then.

The silent child genius raised his hand.

Not that he said anything, mind you—he just held up his hand, but even I could guess what he meant.

He was volunteering to help with the investigation.

And nothing could help an investigation along like the cooperation of Yubiwa—and the Yubiwa Foundation.

The battle of competing theories was falling apart, but it didn't seem to matter anymore—all of us just wanted to find Ms. Towai as soon as possible.

"With Sosaku's help, I believe we can find her by morning."

With his anxiety dispelled and a glimmer of hope in sight, Sakiguchi had regained his confidence, and his voice was back to its beautiful self.

"I see," the leader replied. "In that case, we'll all meet here early tomorrow morning."

Apparently he couldn't even wait till school let out the next day—at times like this he was an elementary school kid through and through.

But he wasn't done.

"Everyone, please redouble your efforts to discover the truth by then. That's your homework."

I got more homework from this detective club than I did from my classes.

If you want to make a jigsaw puzzle more difficult, it turns out increasing the number of pieces isn't the way to do it. No matter how many pieces there are—five hundred, a thousand, ten thousand—the basic task stays the same, and in the end it's only a question of time. Astronauts (yes, the very same profession I aspired to until recently) improve their concentration and perseverance by doing all-white jigsaw puzzles, but even that is only a matter of time in the end.

No, the simplest method for making a puzzle harder, so simple that anyone could do it if they wanted, is to mix in the pieces from another puzzle.

In other words, to do multiple puzzles at once.

This has broken quite a few spirits from what I hear, because the problem is no longer one of time—when two things that appear similar but are actually completely different are mixed together, it really wears a person down.

Sotoin may not have intended to present us with a puzzle like that, but the fact was, he had.

On the one hand was the disappearance of the human subjects from thirty-three canvases, and on the other was the kidnapping of the entire student body from the huge painting in the auditorium. The two mysteries appeared similar, but at root they were entirely different kinds of problems.

Their superficial likeness was what made them so maddening.

Coming up with appropriate—which is to say,

appropriately beautiful—solutions to both problems in the space of one night was way beyond me. After all, I couldn't even claim full ownership of the theory I'd presented earlier in the day.

In which case.

Maybe I ought to call on the wisdom of a certain individual once again.

19. Secret Meeting

On the way home I managed to shake off the delinquent and Mr. Bare-Legs, who tried to see me to my door like they had the previous day.

Trying to run away *before* our meeting was one thing, but I don't think even those two expected me to do it *afterwards*—I got myself alone by telling them I needed to use the ladies' room, then gracefully slipped out the third-floor window.

I'd hit on the idea that adding in the dimension of height might give me an advantage against Mr. Bare-Legs' legs—I think the only reason they didn't come after me was that they foolishly figured they could just lie in wait at the school gate. but even I'm acrobatic enough to jump a wall.

I did it!

This time I'm free!

I gave those snooty pretty boys the slip!

…I was so pleased with myself that I almost forgot

my original goal—my escape may have appeared pointlessly stubborn at first glance, but I did actually have a proper reason for it.

I had to stop somewhere before I went home, somewhere I couldn't bring any other members of the Pretty Boy Detective Club, and so I had to duck out on my two-man escort.

My previous two failed attempts to run away had lacked any real justification—but now that I'd succeeded the third time around, I felt kind of pumped up by my own little Great Escape.

I wondered if the people who escaped their canvases had felt the same way—though I know that's a bit of a crazy thing to say. At the very least, I could hardly imagine the kidnapped students felt as pleased as I did.

Anyway, I headed away from the train station near Yubiwa Academy—and toward a certain bus stop.

This bus stop marked the midpoint between Yubiwa Academy and our traditional rival, Kamikazari Middle School.

But the two schools had butted heads so many times in the past that the midpoint had become more of a middle ground, a sort of demilitarized zone—I guess you could say that like the schools, the bus stop had a history.

Well, even conflicts need rules.

I'll give it more of a grown-up spin and say wars have rules, too—although that statement may be unworthy of a "boy"—but anyway, if a Yubiwa Academy student and a Kamikazari Middle student are going to meet up, the bench at that bus stop is one of the places to do it.

A place that's fair for both parties.

That said, *he* and I had definitely not arranged to meet up—far from it.

He actually had the nerve to say, "I'll be there, but it's fine if you don't come."

It's fine if you don't come.

The guy is a genius.

How the heck did he know that was the surefire way to get me—the girl who comes when she's not invited and runs the other way when she is—to show up?

As soon as he said I didn't need to come, I wanted to.

I *had* to.

Anyway, when I arrived at the bus stop after shaking off my escort, *he*—Fudatsuki—was sitting there as promised.

Lai Fudatsuki.

The student council president of Kamikazari Middle School and recent adversary of the Pretty Boy Detective Club.

20. Concerning Lai Fudatsuki

Just as it's completely inadequate to describe Nagahiro Sakiguchi simply as president of the Yubiwa Academy student council, it's also completely inadequate to describe Lai Fudatsuki simply as president of the Kamikazari Middle School student council.

Fudatsuki is the same age as me, but in addition to being student council president, he's a salesman, a businessman, a manager and an overseer, a producer, a promoter, an investor, a maestro, an impresario, and above all, a playboy.

Among his many ventures, the casino he was running at night in the school gym—the casino we Pretty Boy Detectives unexpectedly got involved with not so long ago—was probably toward the relatively legal end of the spectrum.

With a robust pipeline to a genuine criminal organization, he's an overwhelmingly dangerous individual—although you'd never guess it from his mild manner.

A petit bourgeois like me really has no business getting involved with him, even in the course of my detective work, which is why I had promised myself I would do my best to avoid him at all costs, and which is also why Sakiguchi gave me the kiddy phone. But apparently such defenses were as good as nonexistent to this playboy—worse than nonexistent, actually; he'd called me on that very same kiddy phone, which meant the criminal was using the crime-prevention tools to his advantage.

He'd taken me in.

It was probably pointless to try and figure out how Fudatsuki had gotten ahold of a cell phone number that only members of the Pretty Boy Detective Club were supposed to know—whatever connections or tools he had, this kid drew on essentially bottomless resources.

And he's a second-year middle school student, which is pretty mind-blowing.

But in the end, it all came down to a phone call.

If only I'd hung up sooner, this whole mess would've been over before it started—I should have ignored him, regardless of whether he invited me to meet him or not, whether he said he wanted to see me or not.

The fact that instead of approaching us directly he'd called me to make an appointment beforehand was a sure sign that he felt a certain amount of caution toward the Pretty Boy Detective Club as well. Taking a stronger stand would have been enough to avoid any problems.

"Actually, Ms. Dojima, there's something I'd like from you in return," he'd announced brazenly the night before. "Or perhaps I should say, there's something I'd like you to return to me—remember that money I dropped, which you were kind enough to pick up?"

I knew right away what he was getting at.

I'd been worrying about it myself—I'll skip the details, but picking up his million-yen bundle of banknotes was the catalyst for the showdown between the detectives and the playboy.

We'd boldly infiltrated Kamikazari Middle School in the middle of the night because we felt it would be wrong to accept the ten-percent finder's fee—a hundred thousand yen—which Fudatsuki had given me.

A couple of plot twists later, we'd managed to return sixty thousand out of the hundred thousand yen, but in all the confusion we failed to give back the remaining forty grand, and it had been in my purse ever since—and now Fudatsuki was saying he wanted it back.

After all this time.

"But, well, it's evidence of my crimes, you see. Since I've shut down the casino, I'd like to have it back."

His explanation sounded reasonable—so reasonable, in fact, that it sounded like an excuse. The truth was, he'd scattered "evidence of his crimes" all over the place, and in purely practical terms it was ridiculous to think he'd be able to get back every single one. Plus, the economic foundation he'd built wasn't so unstable that a paltry piece of evidence like that could shake it.

I was certain he had another reason for wanting to meet me—I didn't know what it was, but as a student of Yubiwa Academy, I could hardly respond to an invitation from a guy who was eager to expand the power of Kamikazari Middle without due consideration.

All the same, I couldn't *not* respond—admittedly, as I said before, being told I didn't have to go definitely made me want to, but I'm not such an idiot (I'm not, I swear) that I'd shake off my escort to meet Fudatsuki for that reason alone.

It was also true that I didn't know what to do with that forty thousand yen floating at my fingertips, although if it really bothered me that much I suppose I could have thrown it away—forget evidence, now that the casino was closed the notes were just useless scraps of paper.

But I had to meet up with him.

There was something I had to ask him—again, I won't go into the details, but it had to do with improper activities at the casino he was running.

Improper activities.

I suppose a middle school student running a casino is plenty improper on its own, but he'd been working at something even more improper there.

Although maybe I should say he was playing at something improper—simply put, he'd dramatically increased profits by having an employee in an "invisibility suit" lurking around the casino.

Swindling the guests out of their cash wasn't the point, however—the point, it seems, was to test out the invisibility suit itself. And I'd just happened to uncover the whole thing with my preternatural vision.

It was my first skirmish as Mayumi the Seer, she of the beautiful eyes, member of the Pretty Boy Detective Club.

An immortal moment in my life.

Although mortifying would probably be a more accurate description of my feelings in the moment (never mind guys' clothes, I was wearing a bunny suit, of all things)—but anyway, a few days after it all happened, something occurred to me.

Like, *What the hell?*

Sure, I'm Mayumi the Seer and I have overly good vision, thanks to which I was able to see Fudatsuki's assistant despite some invisibility suit straight out of *Harry Potter*.

I uncovered the presence of a black-clad "kuroko" who was using hand gestures to tell Fudatsuki what cards his opponent held—that much made some kind of sense.

But how on earth had Fudatsuki known what gestures his assistant was making?

After all, the kuroko was wearing invisibility clothes.

Squint as he might, he still shouldn't have been able to see anything—which meant that no matter how much the kuroko gestured, the message should never have gotten through.

Weird.

Contradictory, even.

It was the very definition of not believing one's own eyes.

If it were the plot of a mystery novel, I'd be forced to call it an unacceptable blunder on the part of the author. This was no time to be raising childish questions about the behavior of Nello, the boy from *A Dog of Flanders*—and yet, as a member of the Pretty Boy Detective Club, I needed to come up with a beautiful interpretation like the child genius's. I needed to display my childish boyishness to the fullest.

Judging by the outcome, Fudatsuki had definitely been receiving signals from his assistant in the invisibility suit.

I was forced to conclude that he could see the kuroko—which in turn led me to a hypothesis.

When you have eliminated the impossible, whatever remains, no matter how improbable, must be the truth—in other words.

147

Fudatsuki had it too.

He had the same powers of vision I did.

And if that was true—then I needed to overcome all obstacles, including a pair of tenacious escorts, to see him.

21. Secret Meeting, Part Two

"No, my eyes are exceedingly normal. I do have 20/10 vision in both, but I can't see through objects or see invisible figures. I'm sorry to disappoint you," Fudatsuki said, bowing his head politely.

Bowing his head, but half concealing a smile.

Apparently, he couldn't contain his amusement at my strained logic—crap, he was laughing at me.

I'm the laughingstock of the bus stop as well as the art room.

Had I misread the situation?

But he had to have been able to see the kuroko in the invisibility suit. He had to.

"No no, think about it for a moment. If I had that sort of special vision, I'd have no reason to station an assistant in an invisibility suit behind my opponent, would I? I'd be able to see right through their cards without the need for such an elaborate setup."

"Oh…"

It was true.

Close call.

In attempting to plaster over one contradiction, I'd almost created another.

"In my case, it was less about sight than foresight—I lack your gifts, so I arranged a cunning little scam which relied on tools rather than ability."

He drew a contact lens case from the pocket of his school uniform.

"These lenses render the invisibility suit visible. I wore them during the matches on stage."

"Ohh… So that's how you did it."

The solution was kind of a letdown, but it also made sense—because no matter how those invisibility suits were put to use, if the ones using them couldn't see them either, they wouldn't do much good. It was only natural to test out the technology for seeing through the invisibility technology at the same time you were testing out the invisibility technology itself.

In other words, developing stealth and developing radar were two sides of the same coin. Interesting.

That may have been self-evident to Sakiguchi and the others (if not to the leader), but for the sake of my dignity, I'll ask you to consider it an oversight on my part—literally.

"Of course, the vision these lenses provide is a far cry from your eyesight, Ms. Dojima," he added deferentially.

Fudatsuki may not've had special vision after all, but the fact that he'd brought along those contact lenses suggested he'd nevertheless managed to discern the real reason I had so rashly responded to his invitation.

Yeah, with that kind of insight, you'd hardly need special vision, I thought, feeling dejected.

Dejected? Yes, dejected.

What had I been expecting? Had I really hoped to find someone to share this world with me, the one that only I can see?

I knew perfectly well that the delinquent was right, that there aren't many people like me in this world—but had I still hoped?

Still hoped there was someone out there who'd seen the same star as me?

"I'm sorry to disappoint you," Fudatsuki repeated.

This time without the smile.

"It's fine. My hopes weren't that high anyway... Clearing up that question is more than enough for me."

But I couldn't allow myself to fully accept this shrewd character's explanations. I had to remember that other mysteries related to Fudatsuki's invisibility remained—he hadn't revealed everything.

And that was fine.

I wasn't taking part in this secret meeting as a member of the Pretty Boy Detective Club. I was operating solo, as Mayumi Dojima.

Solo.

All alone, with no one to share the world as I saw it.

"By the way, did my advice come in handy?" Fuda-tsuki asked, changing the subject.

He was clever like that.

A worthy rival indeed for Sakiguchi. He gave the vice president a run for his money when it came to commandeering conversations.

"I wouldn't really say it came in handy, but at least I avoided embarrassing myself. So thanks."

I'm bad at saying thank you.

But I was genuinely grateful.

The night before, when he'd called to invite me to this meeting, I'd offhandedly mentioned my "homework" to him.

"This is just a hypothetical, a what-if, a one-in-a-million, but say there happened to be thirty-three paintings of this, that, and the other in the crawl space above your school's art room, how would you explain it?" I'd asked very naturally, very casually.

And he'd responded with the theory I presented at the meeting earlier that day—what he'd given me was more like coaching than advice.

His theory turned out to be wrong, but it was still way better than having no theory to present at all.

"I see. That is truly unfortunate. I suppose I don't have the makings of a detective after all."

He shrugged. Exactly like a criminal.

He didn't really seem like he thought it was unfortunate at all.

Actually, looking back, I wonder if the whole reason he'd suggested that theory involving eyesight in the first place was to lay the groundwork for inviting me to meet in person—I bet he thought if he said a bunch of stuff about vision, he could get me wondering if he himself had some kind of special vision.

Very naturally, very casually.

Or maybe my imagination was running away with me.

At the very least, I think his second apology was sincere.

"But I must say, I'm surprised to hear that in the course of a single day that pleasant little story you told me turned into a mass kidnapping of the entire student body. I am delighted to know that Yubiwa Academy has had its own share of trials and tribulations."

"Oh, no, that was only another hypothetical, what-if, one-in-a-million kind of story. There was never actually a teacher named Kowako Towai," I said, scrambling to gloss over the truth.

There's no confidentiality clause in the Pretty Boy Detective Club (except on the client side, that is), but I doubt they'd appreciate me blabbering about our activities to the student council president of our rival school.

It wasn't like I was scheming for him to help out with today's homework or anything.

I wasn't, but all I got from him this time was, "Well, if that's the case, then the answer is probably, 'What is essential is invisible to the eye.'"

Just his usual quote from Saint-Exupéry.

Apparently, now that he'd succeeded in luring me out here, he wasn't going to give me any help—in situations like this, he was more businessman than playboy.

Yes, very businesslike indeed.

What is essential is invisible to the eye, eh?

I guess since I can see all kinds of things I don't even want to, that means I get less of the essential stuff than everyone else? And what about Kowako Towai?

What could she see?

What could she not see?

22. Secret Meeting, Part Three

Since my worries (alright, I'll just come out and say it: my hopes. My empty hopes) turned out to be unfounded, I figured I might as well finish carrying out my excuse of an errand, so I ceremoniously handed the envelope containing the four banknotes to Fudatsuki.

"Thank you very much. What a darling envelope."

I just got complimented for my girliness.

How clever of him.

But you won't get much by complimenting a girl dressed as a boy on her girliness, mister.

"This will keep me out of the hangman's noose, thank goodness," he said.

I have no idea how genuinely he meant it.

He was completely different from our leader, who was always genuine—not that I'm saying one is better than the other.

In any case, Fudatsuki had revealed how he'd been able to see the invisible kuroko, and I'd succeeded in my original goal of returning the rest of his dropped cash, so I'd taken care of all the unfinished business from our previous adventure—I think it was safe to say that the case of *The Swindler, the Vanishing Man, and the Pretty Boys*, at least, was closed.

But I had to keep in mind that plenty of other questions still lingered.

"...So are you going around retrieving the money from every single person you handed it out to? You, the maestro, personally?"

"Not necessarily. Our school is blessed with an embarrassment of riches when it comes to human resources—and we're all pulling together to conceal the crime," Fudatsuki replied. "After-sales service, you might say."

By human resources, he probably meant the bunny girls and various other employees who'd been working at the casino—he played it off as a joke, but I think he was genuinely proud of the students at his school.

Although I can't say I approve of concealing crimes.

Is that really the kind of thing you pull together for?

But pointing that out would just be pissing in the wind—the Pretty Boy Detective Club wasn't exactly a law-abiding organization itself.

"However, in your case, I felt I ought to retrieve the bills myself."

"But... why?"

"Why do you think?"

I didn't like having my question answered with a question (I don't like most things), but strangely enough, I didn't feel irritated.

So I answered his question. Defiantly.

"As a pretext. Just like I wanted to see you so I could find out if my hunch was right—"

My hunch about his vision.

My hope that maybe he saw the world as I did.

"—you had some other reason of your own for arranging a secret meeting with me like this. Your real agenda, so to speak."

Fudatsuki narrowed his eyes.

"You're wrong."

Huh?

Here I'd answered like this was some kind of elegant back-and-forth between two people with ulterior motives, but... I was wrong?

He really just wanted the rest of his banknotes back?

"Um... You genuinely didn't have any other reason for seeing me?"

"I did not."

"None at all?"

"None at all."

"Not even one?"

"Not even one."

Fudatsuki had a grin on his face the whole time.

Seriously??

157

But, then, why *hadn't* he left the task up to one of his worthy subordinates? Like that bunny girl who thought I was a guy... Though if she'd been the one inviting me, I don't think I would have shown up no matter how slyly she'd asked.

"I came out personally to meet you, and only you, purely because I wanted to see you, Ms. Dojima. There was no other reason."

So in that sense, you could say the banknotes actually were a pretext, he added smoothly.

So smoothly, in fact, that it almost slipped right by me.

What did he just say? He wanted to see me?

"If you wanted to see me, couldn't you just have ambushed me like before? You hardly needed to set up this little rendezvous."

"Oh, but I wanted to."

"...?"

I didn't get it.

This playboy was a totally different type from the Pretty Boy Detectives, but in this regard, he was a lot like them—he might've even won by a nose in the elusiveness department.

I suppose he couldn't bear to see me so confused, because he kindly put it in simpler terms for me: "You see, for an investor like me, meeting with people like this is all part of the job."

Okay, that did make sense.

Even if he didn't have a specific goal or plan in mind, meeting with people regularly kept him in their minds, and planted the seeds for future dealings.

"In other words, you value my vision, is that right? That's why you came out to meet with me?"

"You can take it that way if you like. An overseer has simply come to meet an over-seer—for now, anyway."

Very suggestive.

Maybe it should come as no surprise for a guy who'd been doing the kind of experiments he had, but Fudatsuki seemed to have a lot of vision jokes up his sleeve.

"So you see, Ms. Dojima, I've already fully achieved my goal—and I hope you'll give me the pleasure of meeting with me again from time to time."

"Uh… I'm not sure about that…" I managed, caught wildly off guard.

I'd returned the banknotes, however belatedly, and I'd unfortunately discovered that Fudatsuki's eyesight was perfectly normal, so as far as I was concerned there wasn't any reason for us to see each other again.

In which case you'd think I would have rejected him a bit more forcefully, but instead I added a vague "Maybe if I feel like it."

I thought my insincere attitude might piss him off, but instead he nodded and said, "That's fine. Frankly speaking, you probably shouldn't even have come here today."

"…"

What the hell? Was he trying to hook me again by pretending he didn't care? Did he really think he could use the same ploy with me over and over now that he knew I'd come if he said I didn't have to?

"What, it didn't occur to you? You didn't think the members of the Pretty Boy Detective Club might feel betrayed that you gave them the slip and went to meet with the top dog of their rival school?"

He kept his voice even, but his sincere tone made it sound a heck of a lot like a lecture.

"Though I suppose it might be easier for you to talk to an enemy you have no need to befriend than to friends you need to be careful around. But we're not the only ones after you… After your vision, that is."

He was right about that.

I couldn't deny the first thing he'd said, and as for the second, he was spot on—I had no idea when the Twenties might pop into my life again.

Which was why I should never give my escorts the slip like I had that day, no matter how urgent the reason.

However.

Willing as I am to do that kind of self-reflection when it's called for, there was one misunderstanding on Fudatsuki's part that I had to correct.

"I don't think I have to be careful around those guys.

I mean, that's the last thing they would want from me. When I want to go somewhere, I go, and when I want to run away, I run away. I say what I want, and I see who I want—and I tell them what I've seen. I can be myself with them."

Friends I don't have to be careful around.

And more than that, friends who aren't careful around me.

That's what I'd always dreamed of—and the Pretty Boy Detective Club was pretty damn close to that ideal.

"Pardon me," Fudatsuki said, standing up from the bench.

I thought this time I must have really pissed him off with my emotional rebuttal, but it seemed he'd only stood up because he saw the headlights of the approaching bus—I guess his only motivation had been to see me after all, and now he was going to get on the bus and that would be that.

For the time being.

His meeting with me was no more than one of the many seeds he planted here and there on a daily basis— just one of the countless little intrigues he wove around himself.

When I thought about it like that, I felt overwhelmed by the scale of his enterprises and embarrassed even to be standing next to him—perhaps, I thought to myself, that was another reason I shouldn't have come to meet him today.

"If you want friends you don't have to be careful around," Fudatsuki cut into my thoughts, looking down at me where I sat on the bench, "then we could also be your friends, Ms. Dojima."

"Um…"

"Come visit our school anytime… If you feel like it. My worthy companions and I—The Heartbreaker Street Irregulars—are ready to welcome you at any time. I'm confident that I can put you to far more appealing use than the Pretty Boy Detective Club."

With those parting words—Fudatsuki stepped onto the waiting bus.

23. You Forgot Something—and Home Again

For a moment I sat there in a daze, but when I suddenly came to my senses I noticed that Fudatsuki had forgotten something on the bench.

His contact lens case.

Which held no ordinary contact lenses, mind you, but those special lenses that allowed him to see the invisibility suit—a dangerous item still in the middle of development and testing.

Fudatsuki had been surprisingly scatterbrained to forget something so important in the midst of his smooth departure—or maybe not.

Maybe he had forgotten them on purpose?

Were they a pretext, or perhaps I should say a seed he had planted in order to arrange another rendezvous with me? It was a fitting promise of a future appointment for a guy who made meeting with people his primary business.

He probably planned to call me up again and say

innocently, "Would you mind giving me back those contact lenses? They're a very important classified item." How perfectly clever of him.

If that was the case, then the proper response might be to pretend I hadn't noticed them and simply return home, but a coward like me lacked the guts to leave some secret military-grade gadget lying around at a bus stop—and so while it infuriated me to knowingly step into a trap, I saw no other option than to go along with Fudatsuki's plan.

I had no choice.

It was my own fault for failing to notice this audaciously forgotten item as Fudatsuki was leaving—although he'd definitely wooed me with that invitation in order to prevent me from noticing.

What had he said? The Heartbreaker Street Irregulars?

I felt like I'd heard that name somewhere before… But anyway, I should probably take his advice seriously.

This time he'd just made a cameo, but that wouldn't necessarily be the case next time around—multifaceted business dealings were his modus operandi, and once he was done tying up the loose ends from his closed casino, there was no telling what he might try to unleash on Yubiwa Academy.

I slipped the "forgotten" contact lenses into the pocket of my blazer and stood up—I lived on a different route, so none of the buses that stopped here would get me home.

But the sky had grown completely dark while I was talking with Fudatsuki, and the nighttime streets are dangerous for a girl walking home alone, even if she is dressed as a boy.

My eyesight renders darkness virtually meaningless, but I could well imagine some ruffians ignorant of that using the night as cover for their bad deeds.

Which is why.

"Sorry to ask when you're hiding and everything, but would you mind walking me home?"

At this, the delinquent emerged slowly from the bushes behind the bus stop where he'd been crouching.

I'd never seen anyone look grumpier in my life.

"Don't tell me you saw through the bushes or something. I didn't see you take off your glasses…"

"Nope, I just figured you were there."

I'd relied on my intuition, not my vision.

I have to admit I knew that the kiddy phone they'd given me was equipped with a GPS lost-kid-finder function, so they wouldn't have much trouble locating me no matter where in the world I ran off to.

If I didn't like it, I could've just turned it off, but I didn't—I wouldn't tell them this, because by this point I'm sure they'd never believe me, but I had never intended to genuinely give them the slip in the first place.

"Where's Mr. Bare-Legs?"

"He went to your house. In case something actually happened."

"Call him then, would you? Tell him his dear friend is alright."

"Demanding, aren't we."

But the delinquent must've felt guilty for listening in on my conversation, because he didn't give me the usual tongue-lashing.

Instead he said, "Next time, I'm gonna make you some *killer* food, so get ready."

Harsh punishment.

"So? What did you and the enemy boss talk about? I couldn't hear much over the sound of the bus there at the end."

"It's a secret."

I can't imagine such a gentlemanly playboy leaving a girl alone on the streets at night, so he must've had an inkling there were other Pretty Boys nearby—which was probably why he'd said the last part under cover of the noise from the bus. With that in mind, I fell into step with the delinquent.

Even now it struck me as strange that I'd felt so embarrassed sitting next to Fudatsuki, but at some point I'd stopped feeling intimidated by being around the outlaw delinquent, who operated on a scale every bit as grand.

24. Early Morning Meeting

I thought that was the end of my little detour from the main story, but afterward I got quite a talking-to from Mr. Bare-Legs.

His lecture was way too serious to call a punchline, more like a bonus chapter you didn't even want at the end of the book—I mean, being furiously dressed down by a younger guy who looks like an angel, who's endlessly bright and playful and usually has a cheerful smirk on his face, is fairly demoralizing, even if you're only a year older.

I still don't get what flips the serious switch on this kid who's been kidnapped three times before.

In any case, after spending three hours sitting contritely in front of my house with my legs folded under me getting yelled at, I hardly had the time or energy left to do the homework Sotoin had given us, so I found myself in the awkward position of heading to school the next morning with no plan whatsoever.

The delinquent had left me in the lurch the second we got there, and Mr. Bare-Legs, being in peak physical condition, seemed to be totally fine with pulling all-nighters. Me, though, I'm the kind of person who generally likes to sleep at night.

I was beyond depressed to think that after finally being dismissed from Mr. Bare-Legs' scolding, I was going to get another lecture the next morning for not doing my homework.

I guess maybe I shouldn't have responded to Fudatsuki's invitation after all—though the reality was that I couldn't very well have turned him down the night before, in which case I should've at least put more pressure on him to give me some advice.

If you're gonna do something, do it right.

Of course, I could easily imagine him casually brushing off my pathetic version of "pressure"... But if I'd kept at him until I at least got a hint, my feet wouldn't feel so heavy on the way to school this morning.

Wait, he might not have given me a hint, but he did say something. Now what was it?

Oh, right, "What is essential is invisible to the eye"—that quote I bet everyone in the world knows, the one from *The Little Prince*.

He said it at the casino, too, so maybe it's his motto?

...Whatever, it didn't matter.

Even the leader, who gave us this homework

assignment in the first place, probably didn't expect much from the newest member of the club.

"Aha! Young Dojima has arrived! Let's hear from you immediately! You always seem to bring new insights that we older members are too stuck in our ways to conceive of! Go ahead now, blow that fresh wind of change into the Pretty Boy Detective Club!"

He expected a ton.

When I arrived, all the other members were already gathered in the auditorium, which was otherwise as empty as the huge painting on the wall—was Mr. Bare-Legs still mad at me? His expression as he watched me walk into the room wasn't exactly how someone looks at a friend.

The delinquent, who knew full well I hadn't had time to come up with any theories, didn't seem to be in the mood to cover for me either—while for his part, the child genius may not have even noticed I'd arrived.

Hey, take a little interest!

Can't you see how desperate I am?

"Well then, since the president has expressed his preference, shall we begin with Ms. Dojima?" said Saki-guchi, who was chairing today's meeting.

Unlike the previous day, when he'd been brooding over his secret, he was ushering things along at a rapid clip—dammit, we're feeling better today, aren't we!

Or maybe the guy with the lolicon had heard about

my secret meeting with Fudatsuki and was torturing me for consulting with his sworn enemy.

So spiteful.

I guess he doesn't just like petite girls, he's a petty person.

I'd been ready to apologize if I had to, but now I felt more like getting my revenge.

"Very well. Please listen quietly as I share with you the true nature of the kidnapping that occurred seven years ago, a theory founded upon firm evidence and sound logic..." I began, pretending to be calm even as my mental gears spun at full speed—it wasn't exactly something to be thinking through on the spur of the moment, but how the hell had Ms. Towai managed to switch out those enormous paintings without being seen?

And method aside... I didn't have a clue *why* she did it, either. It was only natural that she would've been angry about art getting cut from the curriculum, but how would switching paintings help?

It would be one thing if she'd actually kidnapped all the students like the Pied Piper of Hamelin, but...

"Hmm? Whatever is the matter, young Dojima? Your speech stopped just as you were about to reveal the true nature of the situation. Ha ha ha! Never mind being a boy detective, grandstanding like that puts you well into master sleuth territory! Looks to me like you're after a little friendly competition for the title of Kogoro!"

Um, no.

If anyone's after anything little, it's the guy with the lolicon over there.

"Hey, Dojima, that reminds me. You haven't looked at this monster painting with that famous eyesight of yours yet, have you?"

The delinquent must not have been able to stand watching me flounder like that, because he threw me a lifeline—I bestow my praise on you!

But as with the thirty-three canvases we found in the crawl space, all that happened when I took off my glasses was that I saw through the gigantic painting to what was underneath.

A blank white canvas, and behind that a wall. Nothing more.

Needless to say, the wall didn't have any hidden messages inscribed on it or anything—it was just a plain old wall, exactly as advertised.

To say I was confronted by a wall also aptly expresses my mental state—Mayumi the Seer's famous eyesight was useless.

Well, last time it was a bit too useful.

That same eyesight had turned me into a non-functioning human being for ten years—how could I expect it to come in handy every single time I needed something?

"But come now, young Dojima, even grandstanding has its limits! Doesn't this attempt to monopolize the presentation of beautiful theories violate your personal aesthetic?"

I ain't got a personal aesthetic.

Stop hounding the one ordinary person in the club!

Even though I'd stubbornly refused to apologize even after a three-hour lecture from Mr. Bare-Legs, I was on the verge of sinking to my knees when—

"Hurry up and tell us, young Dojima!" the leader urged impatiently. "What sort of theory did you and Fu-datsuki come up with?"

Hold your horses, I'm—wait, even the leader knew about my secret meeting?

I'd totally assumed Michiru's report had only gotten as far as Sakiguchi… And apparently I was right, because Sakiguchi looked as surprised as I was.

Which meant that Sotoin had guessed the truth the day before, when I presented my theory—because that presentation was his only possible grounds for such a deduction.

"Mr. President, y-you knew?" the vice president asked.

"Hmm? That young Dojima had negotiated a beautiful reconciliation with our former enemy, you mean?"

The president sounded just as puzzled as the vice

president.

"There's nothing strange about that. You figured it out yourself, didn't you, Nagahiro?"

Not quite.

Because instead of deductive reasoning, Sakiguchi had used the kiddy phone/dog collar to track my movements. But the leader's words cleanly swept away my guilt at having called on our rival for help with my detective work. And more importantly, they made me feel like I had his support.

A beautiful reconciliation.

Of course, it wasn't really anything like that—but I wanted to reward Sotoin for twisting my rogue actions, the rash behavior that even Fudatsuki himself had scolded me for, into something positive.

Precisely because it wasn't anything like that, that was what I had to make it—I had to make it something beautiful.

Which meant that what they needed from me right now was neither apology nor solicitude.

It was a hypothesis.

A hypothesis worthy of a member of the Pretty Boy Detective Club—worthy of the leader's expectations.

Be beautiful.

Be a boy.

Be a detective.

And—be a team.

"Um… Does anyone…"

Setting aside my pretensions to a speech worthy of a master detective, I timidly raised my hand.

"…know how to put in contact lenses?"

25. Seeing Double

None of the members of the Pretty Boy Detective Club wore contacts, but I suppose these days colored lenses fall within the skillset of a makeup artist, because the child genius volunteered—silently.

He wordlessly acknowledged my presence.

Since I wear glasses to protect my eyes, I'd naturally never put in contact lenses, which is why I asked for help—but forget about how it's done, what we're really talking about is sticking something directly onto your eyeball, which is probably even scarier when someone else does it.

On the other hand, I felt fairly comfortable putting my fate in the child genius's hands, considering he'd already done what he pleased with my nearly naked body the first time he dressed me up as a boy—of course, these were no ordinary contact lenses he was putting in.

These had been left behind by our sworn enemy, with whom I had forged a beautiful reconciliation the night before—custom-made military-grade contacts that artificially endowed their wearer with the ability to "see" invisible clothing.

By no means did I have a specific idea in mind.

No particular prospects, and no notion of the results I might get—if anyone had an idea, it was Fudatsuki.

When I brought up a hypothetical mass kidnapping that had taken place seven years ago, he had offered no advice. I figured that since he had accomplished his professional goal of meeting with me, he wasn't about to give me any more freebies like I'd gotten the previous night.

But what if he had?

Obliquely.

Or, blatantly.

The top dog of Kamikazari Middle School had boasted about putting me to better use than the Pretty Boy Detective Club did, so if he were to give me a helping hand—what form would it take?

The form of a "forgotten" item.

Maybe even the form of a pair of contact lenses—which is why.

After layering the extraordinary contacts over my own exceptional eyes, I looked again at the enormous painting of the empty auditorium.

And then.

I saw right through—to what had really happened.

26. What Really Happened Seven Years Ago

I saw through to what had really happened.

Although I did make one mistaken assumption.

I'd hoped that by layering Fudatsuki's invisi-vision contacts over my own too-good eyesight, I'd double Mayumi the Seer's ability to see through stuff, but in the event, it didn't work like simple addition.

Fudatsuki had said the contacts were nowhere near as good as my own eyesight, but they still improved the wearer's vision enough to render an invisibility suit visible—which is why I thought that if the contact lenses were a "5" and my vision was a "10," adding them together would give me a "15." And maybe if I looked at the giant painting with that boosted vision, I'd see something new.

But 5 plus 10 didn't equal 15—and come to think of it, even with normal glasses that correct your eyesight, putting on two or three pairs at the same time doesn't give you double or triple the benefit.

In this case, the level 5 contacts attenuated my level 10 vision, so I ended up looking at *The Auditorium in the Auditorium* with level 5 vision—which was actually a good thing.

My "too-good eyesight" became "just right eyesight."

My own plan had misfired.

But Fudatsuki's was right on the mark.

"*The painting—wasn't switched out at all,*" I muttered.

Yes.

That was the truth.

"Whaddaya mean it wasn't switched out, Dojima?"

The delinquent gave me a suspicious look.

"We jumped to conclusions," I replied—because yes, that too had been a mistaken assumption.

Of course, it was only natural to assume the painting had been switched out since it was completely different from the original—unlike my silly notion about layering on contacts.

"Gimme a break. If it wasn't switched out, are you saying the students really were kidnapped from the painting?"

"No, that's not it either."

I searched for a clever way to explain it, but no matter how hard I tried, with my paltry vocabulary I could only tell it like it was.

Though that might actually have been the sincerest

attitude I could take toward art, not some string of flowery phrases.

"They've been wholly painted over."

"Wholly…cow!"

Mr. Bare-Legs' mouth dropped open.

Yesss! The shocking truth had softened his anger over my escape, if only a little!

I pressed on, anxious not to let this opportunity go. I was hoping to achieve forgiveness by attrition, which was more a selfish attitude than a sincere one.

"In other words, she altered it from a painting of the whole student body at an assembly to a painting of an empty auditorium—*without ever taking the enormous canvas off the wall.*"

Once you got it, it was obvious.

It was the only possible answer.

If the old canvas couldn't be taken out and a new one couldn't be brought in, there was no other practical solution.

But at the same time, it was a startling breakthrough in our thinking.

If I hadn't seen it *with my own eyes*, I never would have believed it either—that is, if I hadn't looked at the painting with my "attenuated" vision and therefore seen only *halfway* through it, to the "base layer" where the entire student body was lined up in neat little rows, I wouldn't have thought it possible.

I didn't see through to the pure white of the canvas, nor to the empty wall behind it.

Precisely because I only saw through the *topmost layer of paint*—I was able to see the image underneath that had been painted over.

My eyes can see clear through canvas, but I can't control the penetration in a way that would let me see through only that one thin layer of paint—if I could fine-tune my eyesight like that, I wouldn't need protective glasses.

Since he left these contacts behind when he got on the bus, I'm certain Fudatsuki had seen the truth—though not literally.

What is essential is invisible to the eye.

For once, that did appear to be the case.

"Ohh… Now I get it," the delinquent said. "Then, that confirms that the culprit must've been Kowako Towai. Only the artist herself would ever do something as sacrilegious as painting over a finished picture."

I agreed.

When the child genius wanted to tell us that one of the thirty-three paintings was *The Gleaners*, he drew on a picture he'd taken with his phone instead of doing it directly on the canvas—because an artist doesn't paint over another artist's painting.

Ironically, the boldness of the crime pointed straight to the criminal—of course we still had no proof, and it was just a generalization, but I had a hard time imagining that someone capable of painting such a high-quality picture would treat another artist's work with such a lack of respect.

She would never have painted over it.

Unless it was her own.

"Painted over, you say… Yes, if that's the case, it does solve the problems of how she got it in and out of the 'locked room' of the auditorium, how she painted the new picture, and how she disposed of the old one—but, Ms. Dojima," Sakiguchi said, proceeding with the utmost caution.

He seemed to understand that this was the only possible explanation, but still wanted to clear up each and every one of his lingering doubts.

"Look how enormous this painting is. Painting over it would be no mean feat—it must have taken a significant amount of time."

"True, and the original painting took a whole month to complete. It would have been impossible for her to spend that much time working in a public space like the auditorium without being discovered."

"In which case…"

"But she didn't have to repaint the whole thing. The basic composition is the same, so *all she had to do was paint over the rows of students*, which would have reduced her workload by a lot."

"I'll grant you that—but it's still a huge amount of work for one person to do alone."

"What if she wasn't alone?"

From there on out, I was speculating.

Far from staying within the realm of logical deduction, I never even entered it. The original painting had been painted over—that was a fact I had seen with my own eyes, but as for what happened seven years ago, all I could do was rely on my imagination.

All I could do was imagine the most beautiful scenario possible.

"That was the motivation for the kidnapping, so to speak. To carry out this large-scale crime with a large group of people."

"Carrying out the crime with a large group of people was the motivation...? I don't follow you, Ms. Dojima. When you say a large group, who do you mean? Ms. Towai's fellow artists?"

"No, the students of Yubiwa Academy."

It was the only thing that made sense.

Of course, I couldn't rule out the possibility that her fellow artists had helped, but this was the only plausible explanation.

That she, Kowako Towai.

Had recruited the students *she'd taught art to*.

The students who lamented the loss of art class as much as—or maybe even more than—she did, and they'd committed the crime together.

"But Doji, Ms. Towai was a problem teacher, right?"

"Thank you for listening so attentively. That is an excellent question. And those are excellent legs."

I paused in solving the mystery to butter up Mr. Bare-Legs.

I was desperate to get back on his good side.

That was pretty much the same as apologizing, wasn't it?

"But it was only ever the administration who saw her as a 'problem teacher'—from what we've heard, she never abandoned her classes or ignored her students or anything like that."

Sure, holding overseas drawing competitions and modeling nude for middle school students was unquestionably beyond the pale—but even if she'd done lots of things that were problematic for a teacher, as an artist she'd always provided a sterling example for her students. Though maybe that was exactly why she'd been labeled a problem teacher.

And in that case…

Some of the students had to have been on her side.

I hoped so, anyway.

"In the end, the mass kidnapping of seven years ago was Ms. Towai's final class—even if all the students in the school didn't attend, I think she taught the ones who did everything she could by painting alongside them."

The techniques of a painter, of course, but also what it means to be an artist.

Fudatsuki, who greatly values the planting of seeds, would probably say she was simply motivated by a playful heart—but in any case, Ms. Towai had planted seeds in the hearts of the children.

Seven years had passed since then.

The students who were in their first year of middle school at the time were about twenty years old now— what sorts of adults had they become?

Ms. Towai's goal had been nothing so narrow-minded as revenge for her firing—no, she'd had her eyes on the future.

I looked at the child genius.

He'd probably known the truth from the start.

Even without my eyesight or Fudatsuki's contacts, someone with the right expertise could probably tell if a picture had been painted over—so, conversely, the fact that no one outside the group who had participated in the act seven years ago had ever guessed the truth meant they had no eye for art.

"I think the reason Ms. Towai disappeared seven years ago wasn't that she wanted to turn her back on the world, it was that she wanted to take sole responsibility for the crime. She wanted to make sure there was no way the students who had worked alongside her would be punished."

Maybe I was giving the problem teacher a little too much credit, but at the same time, it all made sense.

And who knows, maybe some school employees did guess the truth. There had to be at least a few who got where she was coming from—but they probably would've kept quiet, and even if not, with so many students involved in the crime, they would've had no choice but to cover it up.

The crime probably wasn't all that calculated—though on second thought, that kind of thorough planning might actually be second nature to an artist.

"Beautiful," Sotoin murmured.

That was all.

But even though it wasn't as if he'd said it to praise me, for some reason I felt suddenly bashful, and added, "W-Well, anyway, I'm not sure how much of it is true."

"All of it," a voice declared.

I turned around.

Kowako Towai was standing in the doorway of the auditorium.

27. Confession

"Ha ha ha. Of course, part of it was plain old disgust with the school—it's a crying shame I never painted their crying faces, those bums."

Logic can't explain how I knew instinctively that she was Kowako Towai. I'd only been at the school for a year, so I didn't know what she looked like, and I'd never seen a photo of her—but something about the way she was standing there left no room for doubt.

Even without that, I would probably have been able to deduce she was an artist from her paint-splattered clothes and the handkerchief wrapped around her head.

She looked like she'd walked straight from her studio into the auditorium, totally indifferent to her appearance—and while that made it hard to tell how old she was, she looked quite a bit younger than I'd imagined.

Her face was so covered in paint that I couldn't say

for sure, but judging from the way Mr. Bare-Legs perked up when he saw her, she was probably a beauty underneath it all.

"...Are you Ms. Towai?"

Unlike me, Sakiguchi—who'd been tracking her whereabouts with the help of the child genius—probably recognized her face, but he asked nonetheless.

"Indeed I am," she replied with a puckish air. "I'm Kowako Towai. Former teacher, current artist, and kidnapper of the hour."

"..."

The sudden appearance of the artist, who sounded totally unabashed, seemed to have caught Sakiguchi off guard as well.

I'd been certain he was the one who had asked her to come, since he'd been investigating her whereabouts, but apparently not—we now had the unexpected opportunity to confirm our solution, but if Sakiguchi hadn't invited her, why was she here?

The criminal always returns to the scene of the crime.

You hear that a lot, but would someone really come back after seven years? And just when we were in the middle of investigating the crime? That would be quite the coincidence.

"Sure would. Anyway, they really hate me around here, so the truth is, I didn't want to come—but I heard some kids had the nerve to commandeer my art room even though it was supposed to be locked up. That you?"

She was grinning the whole time.

There was a certain, how can I put it, pressure behind that smile.

But nonetheless, the leader answered boldly, "Yes, that's us. We are the Pretty Boy Detective Club."

"Funny name."

She walked toward us as she continued. "So, did you solve the other mystery?"

She looked at me like she was testing me.

The other mystery?

Oh right, I'd forgotten.

That was where all of this had started—the art room.

The thirty-three paintings we found in the crawl space of what Ms. Towai had called "my art room."

The paintings copied sans their human subjects.

Our search for the meaning behind those paintings had kicked everything off.

"Unlike when we painted over this huge canvas, I did those all by myself. What do you think my motivation was?"

Hell of a way to beat around the bush.

It was easy to see how people might dislike her.

Talking to children this way the first time she met them would probably disqualify her from being a teacher as far as most people were concerned—but for a master speaking to her apprentices, even if they were children, taking an unsparing attitude right from the start might be just the thing.

I couldn't play the good apprentice, though.

Because I'd forgotten all about the other mystery—and it wasn't like solving the mystery of the huge painting in the auditorium automatically led to solving the mystery of the art room.

They were completely separate.

Even after you've sorted the mixed-up puzzle pieces into two piles, you're still more or less at square one.

But I sensed Ms. Towai wasn't so lenient as to let me get away with saying I didn't know—so I just stood there, completely stymied.

"Our resident artist will answer that question," the leader interjected, clapping the child genius on the back. "Speak up, Sosaku."

It wasn't just me; Sakiguchi, the delinquent, and Mr. Bare-Legs all looked startled too—none of us had expected that from the guy who always spoke for the child genius.

Even the child genius himself was probably caught off guard—but while his expression didn't flicker, he did resolve to speak.

"It's not that you didn't paint the people."

In a bold break with customary practice, he was

speaking for the second time in the course of a single case.

"It's that you painted the gods."

28. The Truth Behind the Crawl Space

She didn't not paint people, she painted the gods.

If I'd heard that thoroughly confounding statement the night before, I'm sure I would've been totally baffled—it probably would've only served to fuel my confusion.

But now that the mystery of the giant painting in the auditorium had been solved, and Ms. Towai herself was standing there before us, those few words were enough.

Anyone could see that there were no human figures depicted in those thirty-three canvases, of course—the people had been removed from the masterworks each painting was based on, there was no other way to interpret it.

But at the same time, you could put it differently.

The artist had painted everything *other than* the human beings.

Other than the human beings.

Landscapes, scenery, nature, plants and animals,

angels and deities.

There was no shared element whatsoever among the thirty-three wildly varied paintings, and the artists and eras were all over the place. No shared element—or so it seemed.

But once you noticed a premise so fundamental it could hardly even be called a unifying theme—the presence of human figures in all of the original paintings— then the artist's intentions also came into view.

The thirty-three paintings had been chosen *specifically in order to not paint human figures*—or to put it the other way around, the chances that the artist had chosen them because she didn't like to paint people or was bad at it were vanishingly slim.

Because if that were the case, she could simply have copied paintings that didn't have people in them to begin with—but she hadn't.

Ms. Towai had exclusively chosen paintings with people in them—and then asked them to withdraw from the locked rooms of the canvases.

And the point of it all?

It wasn't about the humans who had been removed—it was about the locked rooms that had been left behind.

"So…you're saying she did it because she hated people?" Mr. Bare-Legs asked, tilting his head quizzically. But that wasn't it.

Of course, you had to be pretty warped to try an experiment like that, but Ms. Towai wasn't a plain old misanthrope—after all, she'd painted every single student at the school into *The Auditorium in the Auditorium* all by herself, which made me tired just thinking about it.

What we had to focus on now was what the thirty-three canvases had in common, the shared element that we'd previously decided didn't exist—no, you know what, we were right. It didn't exist after all.

It really just boiled down to a question of Ms. Towai's tastes.

But her tastes alone didn't explain the issue Sotoin had raised—it was unimaginable that she wouldn't have included Leonardo da Vinci's *Mona Lisa* when she set out to choose her subjects. And maybe Munch's *The Scream* as well.

There were probably others, too—I could think of plenty of paintings whose absence from the collection seemed strange.

Then what did *they* share?

What did the paintings she hadn't chosen have in common?

Landscapes, nudes, historical paintings, genre paintings, war scenes, Japanese paintings, ink wash paintings, abstracts… The thirty-three canvases included all kinds of artists and eras, styles like Impressionism and Cubism, even a variety of media from oil paintings to watercolors to woodblock prints. Yes, they all depicted human figures, but what did the historically important works she *hadn't* chosen have in common?

It was obvious.

It became obvious as soon as I envisioned all thirty-three paintings—Ms. Towai hadn't selected any *self-portraits*, no matter how famous or how universally recognized they were as masterpieces.

There were portraits, but no self-portraits—so to take it a bit further, she hadn't painted any paintings of artists.

When she removed the human beings from all manner of paintings spanning genre and era, East and West, she made an exception for the tribe of artists—because they were exceptional.

It was as if.

She was likening the great artists to gods.

…If that was the case, then it explained the absence of the *Mona Lisa*. There's a popular belief—probably apocryphal, but so widespread that even I've heard of it—that Leonardo's *Mona Lisa* is actually a self-portrait. And no matter how unreliable that rumor might be, if there was even a one-in-a-million chance it was true, she would want to avoid the risk of accidentally eliminating that universal genius from the canvas.

Munch's case is even more cut and dried.

Although you can't really call it a self-portrait, *The*

Scream is the artist's depiction of his own terror at the scream of nature—in other words, the central figure is Munch.

If she had made studies of those two works, she would have been forced to paint them as they were, and the theme of her series would have lost its meaning.

Her theme.

That is—her faith.

She expressed that faith not by deifying artists in her paintings, but by choosing not to paint people who weren't artists—and while it may have been twisted as a mountain path, the impartiality of that choice to ultimately paint neither artists nor non-artists was also an act of tenderness. So if she had chosen a work by Leonardo or Munch, it would've had to be something other than the *Mona Lisa* or *The Scream*.

When the child genius said there were at least thirty-three more canvases, he must've been thinking of the self-portraits by the artists who painted the first thirty-three—and needless to say, she wouldn't have removed the great artists from those paintings.

But her versions of those paintings didn't actually exist.

Her approach wasn't "I don't paint what I can't paint," but rather "I paint what I want to paint by not painting it."

The images of those figures Ms. Towai worshipped

weren't in any crawl space; they existed only on the canvases of her heart—

"Come on, come on, stop it. Enough already."

Up to this point Ms. Towai had been acting so brazenly that you'd never guess she was a trespasser, but all of a sudden she was flapping her hand in embarrassment.

"I never imagined you'd guess the truth," she said. "I figured I'd just get a good laugh out of whatever cockamamie answers you came up with. Damn, if I'd known you were going to embarrass me like this I never would've come." But there was a redness in her cheeks that had nothing to do with the paint all over her face, and she looked somehow pleased.

"You, what's your name?" she asked the child genius.

He had returned to silent mode, however, so Sotoin answered for him.

"Sosaku Yubiwa. We call him Sosaku the Artiste, creator of beauty."

But he didn't stop there.

"He's the heir to the Yubiwa Foundation, the same organization that chased you out of this school."

Um, I think that qualifies as TMI?

But maybe he thought it wouldn't have been fair to conceal that information from her—maybe it would have violated his aesthetic.

Ms. Towai nodded with a chuckle, and just said, "Is he now? If a guy like you had been around seven years ago, maybe I wouldn't have gotten the axe."

Short and sweet.

I'm pretty sure her attitude was genuine, but I also imagine her life as a teacher seven years ago felt like ancient history at this point.

"...There's one thing I still don't get," the delinquent broke in.

I was suddenly overtaken by the desire to point out that there was likely a lot more than one thing he didn't get, but I restrained myself—I'm not that low.

"I get now why you painted those pictures, but why'd you hide 'em in the art room crawl space when they fired you?"

Oh yeah. That mystery still wasn't solved.

Those canvases were an expression of her inner self, so how come she'd left them in the art room? Don't tell me she simply forgot them or something?

No.

Just like Fudatsuki hadn't really forgotten those contact lenses on the bench, there was no way those thirty-three paintings just got left behind by accident.

"No, I mean... There's no deeper meaning to it."

She wiped her hands with the kerchief wrapped around her head—which was probably another attempt to cover up her embarrassment.

"I imagined if I hid them in the crawl space, somewhere down the line when the art room was being used

197

again, some weird kids might find my paintings—and I wanted them to be like, 'What the hell are these?'"

I bet she never thought it would actually happen.

I bet she thought the art room would never be used again, and even if it were, no one would make a point of inspecting the ceiling, and if for some other reason the paintings were discovered, no one would think twice about tossing them in the trash.

No matter what kind of artist she was, no one could've expected this.

That seven years later, a crazy bunch of kids would commandeer the art room, discover the canvases in the course of painting a mural on the ceiling, take them down and think, "What the hell are these?" and end up getting pulled into the mystery just like she'd planned.

"You the one that found them, Sosaku Yubiwa?"

"Young Dojima was the one who discovered them. Mayumi the Seer, she of the beautiful eyes," Sotoin said, kindly introducing me to the artist.

"Yeah? She's the one who solved the mystery of *The Auditorium in the Auditorium*, too, wasn't she? Must be some kind of child genius."

Um, no. That's Sosaku.

And anyway, it was mostly thanks to borrowed wisdom that I was able to solve the mystery at all.

"This is Michiru the Epicure, he of the beautiful palate, otherwise known as Michiru Fukuroi. This is Hyota the Adonis, he of the beautiful legs, otherwise known as Hyota Ashikaga. And this is Nagahiro the Orator, he of the beautiful voice, otherwise known as Nagahiro Saki-guchi."

Sotoin introduced our members one by one—looking genuinely pleased as he did so.

"And who are you?"

"Manabu Sotoin. Manabu the Aesthete, lover of beauty, president of the Pretty Boy Detective Club. I think it's a wonderful thing that a teacher like you was here seven years ago. And I'm delighted to have met you today," he replied.

I assumed he was delighted because we'd been able to promptly confirm the accuracy of our theories, but it wasn't so.

"You see, there's a favor I'd like to ask of you," he continued. "Ms. Towai, it's your art room. But as a reward for solving the mystery, would you be willing to pass it on to us? The Pretty Boy Detective Club would like to carry on your beautiful vision."

Epilogue

And so, by solving the mystery, a band of rogues who had commandeered an unused classroom came to properly inherit the facilities from their former occupant, thus officially turning the art room at Yubiwa Academy into the headquarters of the Pretty Boy Detective Club—and I should probably end this tale right there, but I'm sorry to say there are still one or two more lilies I need to gild.

My approach is the polar opposite of Ms. Towai's, who expressed respect for artists by not painting them, but I must say that wanting to gild lilies is painterly in its own way, and by the strained logic that most people would consider a golden lily an evolutionary advance, I'd like to tack on seven more pages.

First, let me address the last mystery in need of solving.

We had managed to come up with solutions to the mystery of the thirty-three paintings in the crawl space and the giant painting in the auditorium which were, if not precisely true, at least beautiful. But the question remained of how Ms. Towai, who had painted all those paintings and generously confirmed our theories, had appeared in the auditorium with such impeccable timing.

Why did the legendary teacher who disappeared seven years ago return to the school at precisely that moment?

I couldn't possibly set down my pen without addressing that mystery—there's no way she was simply waiting in the wings for her cue.

She'd played it off by saying, "I heard some kids had the nerve to commandeer my art room," but if that was true, who'd she hear it from?

Sakiguchi and the child genius had more or less pinned down her whereabouts in the course of their long evening's investigation, but they hadn't yet had a chance to contact her. I suppose they'd planned to take the helicopter there once we'd solved the mystery or something—so it was probably a good thing for everyone that she showed up when she did.

But then, who'd tattled on us?

I don't know.

I don't know, but I do know someone who was aware that the Pretty Boy Detective Club was searching for a former teacher and current artist by the name of Kowako Towai—because I had told him so at the bus stop.

What I can say about the guy who so conspicuously left his contacts on the bench is that meetings are his business, he knows a lot of people, and he has close ties with the Twenties, a criminal organization that will "transport" anything and anyone anywhere their clients want.

Which means that drawing on his personal network—his contacts, so to speak—to find a missing person and (assuming she was still alive) transport her to and from a certain middle school auditorium should have been a piece of cake.

But…he didn't have any reason to do so, and even if he did, it wasn't hard to imagine how the petty guy with the lolicon would react to hearing that his younger rival had beaten him at his own game, so maybe it's best to leave this particular mystery unsolved.

Maybe that would be the beautiful thing to do.

As it happens, Sakiguchi's ultimately pointless search for Ms. Towai apparently led him to an otherwise uninhabited island, so small it wasn't even on the map—where I hear she's still living a self-sufficient life devoted to her art.

No wonder no one could find her.

Happily, our case hadn't taken us to this place whose neighbors apparently refer to it as a modern-day Panorama Island, but Ms. Towai invited us to visit her there any time we liked. Ha ha ha, like that's ever gonna happen.

And one last bonus:

A few days later, the child genius finished his mural.

It covered the whole ceiling, rivaling Ms. Towai's giant painting in scale. And thanks to the combined efforts of the Pretty Boy Detective Club, we finished well ahead of schedule.

Who knows, maybe the child genius was also inspired by his encounter with Kowako Towai.

If only a person with Yubiwa's artistic sensitivity had been working at the school seven years ago—Ms. Towai had said that, but I suppose he won't be able to devote himself to art forever.

As heir to the Yubiwa Foundation, he's already involved in its management, and eventually he'll have to shoulder the job in earnest—so the day will inevitably come when he has to give up his art.

Maybe that's why he took part with such uncharacteristic enthusiasm in this case, speaking more than once, even.

Maybe that's why he's a member of the Pretty Boy Detective Club—because he, more than anyone, longs to be a boy and not a man.

I was afraid to take the contacts out myself, so I had him help me again, and I took the opportunity to ask him a question.

"Hey, child genius, what motivated you to paint the ceiling?"

Naturally, he didn't answer.

Fine by me, I'm used to it.

Later, while I was passing up paints to him, the scale was so massive I couldn't even tell what he was painting, let alone why.

No one would tell me, either.

"Dear, dear, is this really the same Ms. Dojima who so recently demonstrated such masterful powers of deduction?" Sakiguchi teased, after which I lost my appetite for asking any more questions.

Come on, you know better than anyone how little that had to do with my own abilities.

Apparently, he didn't like that I'd leaned on his sworn enemy for help, regardless of the fact that I had the leader's blessing. Whatever, there's no harm in being resented by a guy with a lolicon.

But as the monumental mural neared completion, the whole picture gradually came into focus.

Over (under?) a background of pure black sprawled all eighty-eight of them.

The huge bear and lion stood out, so at first I thought he had painted a safari scene, but no—there was a goat with the bottom half of a fish, and a chameleon.

There was a picture of someone's hair, and another of a water jar.

A scorpion and a serpent.

A maiden and a god.

He had painted the eighty-eight constellations.

A picture of the heavens that even a planetarium could never manage.

I stood there staring up at the completed painting with my mouth hanging open.

"Ha ha ha! I'm delighted to see it pleases you, young Dojima! Your happiness is a fitting reward for Sosaku, since he painted it for you!" Sotoin said, laughing joyfully—he painted it for me?

I looked around for the child genius, thinking I must've misheard; his work complete, I found him sitting on the sofa with Mr. Bare-Legs and Sakiguchi, sipping a cup of the delinquent's tea.

"Now that we've got this colossal painting on the ceiling, even gloomy old Dojima might look up now and then," the delinquent said brusquely, not exactly speaking for the child genius as he set my tea on the table.

"..."

In response, I looked up at the ceiling again—yes.

I'd stopped looking at the night sky when I lost sight of the phantom star I'd spent ten years chasing—I'd lost the desire to look up.

That's why I joined the Pretty Boy Detective Club.

So I could look at the sky again one day.

"You did all this...for me?" I said in disbelief to no one in particular.

"What are you talking about, Doji? You did it with

205

us," Mr. Bare-Legs said from his upside-down position on the sofa—apparently working together on the mural had done away with the last of his anger.

He was right.

Just like Ms. Towai had made the students her accomplices in the mass kidnapping, I'd played an admirable supporting role in recreating the starry sky on the ceiling of the art room.

"And we did it with the permission of the former owner. I'm so glad we were able to bring the mural to fruition without any cause for further hesitation," Sakiguchi chimed in, in his beautiful voice.

Well, technically speaking, Ms. Towai had only been using a room that belonged to the school, so it wasn't quite accurate to call her the former owner—but when I realized that was one reason Sakiguchi had worked so hard to track down Ms. Towai, I felt genuinely bad about meeting with his sworn enemy behind his back (even if that's not how I thought of it at the time) and calling him "the guy with the lolicon" over and over. I think I'll give him my elementary school uniform to make it up to him—assuming he's satisfied with mine, that is.

"Ha ha ha! Young Dojima, until the day you once again look up at the real night sky, I invite you to enjoy these beautiful stars to your heart's content! And I will accept the pleasure of joining you! Alright then, lads, once you've finished your tea, it's time to prepare for a

206

party! Let us make merry in honor of completing this great work of art!"

With that, the leader nudged me toward the sofa— we talk about things being beautiful beyond description, beyond depiction.

And yet I wished someone would paint a picture of that moment, all of us looking up at the same scene, when I felt for the first time like I'd truly become one of them.

Afterword

It's hard to believe today, but when Edogawa Rampo's famous story "The Stalker in the Attic" was first published, reviews were surprisingly lukewarm. Which is to say, it came in for quite a bit of criticism. This might sound a little too pat, and I can't blame anyone for being dubious, but after all, you do hear similar stories in every field: Vincent van Gogh's paintings hardly sold at all until after his death, Sir Arthur Conan Doyle wasn't very fond of Sherlock Homes, when I reread my first novel it's so embarrassing, that melody is just something I came up with on the spot, etcetera, etcetera. Neither the intent of the author nor the opinion of the reader is necessarily set in stone, and the two don't always line up. They shift with time and chance, making a definite, absolute assessment a rare commodity in the arts. This raises the question of how many masterpieces have been buried over the years, which in turn makes me feel kind of overwhelmed. Some works of art find no public favor whatsoever thanks to nothing more than bad luck, while in other cases the artist has a flash of genius but decides it's not quite there, and rejects the idea before it ever sees the light of day. The truth is, such cases probably represent the majority. When you think about it that way, the works that have managed to survive a hundred, two hundred, a thousand, even two thousand years seem all the more remarkable.

Which brings me to the Pretty Boy Detective Club's third case file. Mayumi Dojima seems to be fitting in quite well with the other detectives by this point, don't you think? This installment put the spotlight on Sosaku the Artiste, aka Sosaku Yubiwa. The silent artistic genius, with a gift for management as well… Though he himself may wish he only had one of those talents. They say the gods don't give with both hands, but when they do, it gets complicated; the receiver is apt to go astray and get stuck vacillating between two options, unable to choose either one. So in that spirit, this has been volume three of the *Pretty Boy* series, *The Pretty Boy in the Attic*.

Thank you, Kinako, for being kind enough to give us a picture of Sosaku and Hyota for the cover. Readers, I sincerely hope you'll join me again for the next volume.

NISIOISIN

Prolific and palindromic NISIOISIN won the 2002 Mephisto Prize at the age of only twenty for his debut mystery novel *Decapitation: Kubikiri Cycle*. Since then he has penned more than one hundred novels across numerous series, many of which have been adapted for manga and television. He is one of the best-selling Japanese authors in recent memory, and has been hailed for breaking down the barriers between mainstream literary fiction and so-called light novels.

KIZUMONOGATARI WOUND TALE
PRINT | 354 PAGES | $14.95 | 9781941220979
AUDIO | 9.5 HOURS | $19.99 | 9781942993940

FIRST SEASON

BAKEMONOGATARI
MONSTER TALE 01
240 PAGES | $13.95
9781942993889

BAKEMONOGATARI
MONSTER TALE 02
328 PAGES | $14.95
9781942993896

BAKEMONOGATARI
MONSTER TALE 03
224 PAGES | $13.95
9781942993902

AVAILABLE NOW!

NISEMONOGATARI
FAKE TALE 01
304 PAGES | $15.95
9781942993988

NISEMONOGATARI
FAKE TALE 02
296 PAGES | $15.95
9781942993995

NEKOMONOGATARI
CAT TALE
(BLACK)
288 PAGES | $15.95
9781945054488

© NISIOISIN/KODANSHA

EKOMONOGATARI CAT TALE (WHITE)

PRINT | 304 PAGES | $15.95 | 9781945054495
AUDIO | 7.5 HOURS | $23.99 | 9781949980035

AND MORE FROM

**KABUKIMONOGATARI
DANDY TALE**

322 PAGES | $15.95
9781945054846

**HANAMONOGATARI
FLOWER TALE**

290 PAGES | $15.95
9781947194069

**OTORIMONOGATARI
DECOY TALE**

290 PAGES | $15.95
9781947194144

THE SECOND SEASON!

**ONIMONOGATARI
DEMON TALE**

290 PAGES | $15.95
9781947194311

**KOIMONOGATARI
LOVE TALE**

290 PAGES | $15.95
9781947194335

THE ZAREGOTO NOVELS—
NISIOISIN'S STARTING POINT

A dropout from an elite Houston-based program for teens is on a visit to a private island. Its mistress, virtually marooned there, surrounds herself with geniuses, especially of the young and female kind—one of whom ends up headless one fine morning.

DECAPITATION
KUBIKIRI CYCLE
The Blue Savant and the Nonsense User

US $14.95 / $17.95 CAN | 9781945054211

© NI

STRANGULATION
KUBISHIME ROMANTICIST
No Longer Human -
Hitoshiki Zerozaki

US $14.95 / $17.95 CAN | 9781945054839

SUSPENSION
KUBITSURI HIGH SCHOOL
The Nonsense User's Disciple

US $14.95 / $17.95 CAN | 9781947194892